THE HONORABLES
A NOVELLA

TRUTH
WITHIN
Dreams

Elizabeth Boyce

Bestselling author of *Honor Among Thieves* and *Once a Duchess*

Crimson Romance
New York London Toronto Sydney New Delhi

CRIMSON
ROMANCE

Crimson Romance
An Imprint of Simon & Schuster, Inc.
1230 Avenue of the Americas
New York, NY 10020

ISBN 978-1-4405-8499-2
ISBN 978-1-4405-8500-5 (ebook)

To Mahala, my cohort in many an ill-conceived scheme.

Acknowledgments

Mega thanks to Tara Gelsomino, Julie Sturgeon, and Jess Verdi, the Crimson Romance triumvirate of awesome. Thanks, too, to my copyeditor, Annie Cosby, who has an incredible eye (and memory!) for detail. Deep appreciation goes to the art department at Crimson, who never fail to make my stories the prettiest books on the block.

Sarah and Michelle, thank you for keeping me sane and on track. To my SCWW writing group, thank you for the many years of friendship and critiques. A heart full of gratitude to The Oasis for always cheering me on and spreading the good word. You ladies (and Jim!) are the very best.

Finally, a big thank you to my family, near and far. Spouse, parents, siblings, kids, inlaws, and cousins—I love you all and couldn't do this without you. This go around, Patty wins first place for Most Enthusiastic Support. The rest of you, try harder next time.

Prologue

"That's never happened with a woman before."

Henry De Vere sat on the edge of the bed, clutching the counterpane to his chest, and aimed this pronouncement over his shoulder to the woman whose gaze was drilling into his bare back.

The weight of her attention was oppressive, and Henry couldn't get a handle on it. Did she pity him? Hate him? Was she waiting for him to leave the room so she could burst out laughing?

He couldn't quite bear turning to look at her. It was possible he'd never be able to look at another human being again. "I'm sorry about your slippers."

There was a pregnant pause from the other side of the bed.

Finally, she broke the silence. "Will you be paying for my shoes, or should I bill your friend?" Her speech, Henry noted, had regained its cultured tones. A few minutes ago, he'd awakened to her screeching at him in a northern dialect he'd had trouble deciphering.

Embarrassment swarmed his skin like bees crawling all over him, itchy and hot, stinging his ears, making them burn. "I'll pay for them," he muttered.

When she spoke again after another miserable stretch of quiet, her voice was husky, amused. "You'd be surprised, the things I see in my profession."

Considering this, Henry frowned. It was the first direct reference she'd made to her line of work. Henry knew what she was, of course, but he hadn't wanted to think of her as a courtesan who received payment in exchange for her favors. He'd enjoyed fancying himself as a virile stallion, whose potent masculinity she'd been powerless to resist. But maybe … maybe it was better this way. After all, she *was* a professional, and therefore, probably encountered her fair share of physical impairments. The knot between his shoulder blades eased a fraction.

"So," he said, watching his toe trace the pattern in the rug, "you've seen this before?"

Silence again.

How had those blasted bees managed to get behind his eyeballs? Henry blinked against the hot prickles.

"How old are you, Mr. De Vere?" she asked. "Lord Sheridan mentioned it was your birthday."

"Nineteen," he whispered, not trusting his voice not to crack.

A few months back, Sheri had written to Henry in his feverishly excited way when he'd first made the acquaintance of Kitty Newman, an exclusive London courtesan whose usual clients included the highest members of Society. Sheri's warped mind had decided that a glorious night with Kitty would be the ideal birthday present for his younger friend. Using an intricate machinery of social connections and favors Henry didn't understand, Sheri had managed to procure Kitty's services for the occasion. She'd even traveled to Oxford to spend the night with Henry in a little house owned by another of Sheri's well-heeled friends.

"Nineteen," Kitty mused aloud. "By my nineteenth birthday, I was already mistress to a minor member of the Swedish royal family. He bought me a pleasure yacht. Now look at me." She sighed.

The assignation had started well enough. Henry had presented himself at the appointed time, a fistful of flowers clutched in a sweaty palm and stomach cramping with nerves. To his surprise, Kitty had led him not to the bedroom, but to a little sitting room, where they'd chatted over a glass of sherry.

Kitty Newman wasn't at all what Henry had expected from a courtesan. She'd asked about his studies, and what he liked to do in his free time. They'd discussed books they'd both read, and she'd told him about an art exhibition she'd recently attended.

The dress she wore was fashionable, but nothing his admittedly uneducated eye would call risqué. Altogether, that first hour felt very much like many he'd spent in the company of other ladies, in other sitting rooms. Specifically, he thought of the Baxters, his neighbors back home. Lady Baxter always asked after his studies, too, while insisting he have another biscuit and simultaneously discouraging Claude, her youngest son and two years his junior, from finishing the entire plateful. Meanwhile, Claudia, Claude's twin, pressed him for tales of the things he'd seen and done in Oxford and London. Her pleasure at his recitations never failed to make him feel worldlier than he really was.

Thinking of Claudia, a sudden pang of homesickness, such as he'd not experienced in a long time, needled through his chest.

"Was I your first, Mr. De Vere?"

He nodded.

Behind him, the bedclothes rustled. "I suspected."

More silence followed. She didn't say precisely *why* she suspected his inexperience, but he must have been too … something … during their copulation. Eager, perhaps. Lacking finesse. And now she'd laid bare the lie in his stupid, stupid statement: *That's never happened with a woman before.* Of course not. *Nothing* had ever happened with a woman before.

A thought, no more than an earthworm of hope, nosed to the surface of his consciousness. "Being the first time, maybe that's why … it … happened." He couldn't bring himself to specifically articulate his disgrace. "Perhaps it wouldn't happen again."

"Perhaps," she said, her dubious tone neatly plucking that lowly worm out of the earth and leaving it to bake in the unforgiving sun. She was being charitable, treating him like a child who needed placating, which only compounded his mortification.

All Henry wanted to do was get away. His clothes lay scattered across the floor. To collect them, he'd have to stand up, expose himself again. He didn't know if he could do that. Hadn't he exposed himself enough for one night?

But he couldn't just continue sitting here, either. If he wasn't going to get back into bed with Kitty (and he wasn't), then he had to take action.

Henry tried several mental tricks to motivate himself. First, he imagined his elder brother, Duncan, standing in the corner, his thin upper lip curled in disdain. *For God's sake*, he could hear his brother snap, *you're a disgrace to the De Vere name. Act like a man, why don't you.*

Henry's lip curled. "Act like a man, why don't you," he mocked under his breath. "Shut up, Duncan."

"Beg your pardon?" said Kitty. "Did you say something?"

"No, no, nothing," Henry assured her.

Quickly, he thought of The Honorables, his group of close friends. The other four men would offer a variety of responses to his predicament, from good-natured laughter to a sympathetic slap on the back. None of those seemed very comforting right now.

He twisted his shoulders; his skin still felt wrong, and his stomach hurt. That little stab of homesickness he'd felt before returned. It wasn't his own home, Fairbrook, he missed, but Rudley Court, for which he longed. There had been nothing wrong with his own home, per se, but the happiest times of his childhood had been spent with the Baxters, free and accepted in a way he'd never quite experienced at Fairbrook. A dose of that loving acceptance would be most welcome right now.

While sitting there, on a borrowed bed in a borrowed house with a borrowed woman, Henry thought wistfully of tree forts and foot races, picnics and riding, charades and dancing lessons. And he yearned.

All you have to do is step through that door, he told himself, *and you'll be there.* He could picture it now, an endless summer day at Rudley Court spent with Claude and Claudia, the people he might just love best in the world, alongside The Honorables. In his imagination, they were all children again, and everything was easy and fun.

With his mind's eye full of lily pads and skipping stones, Henry released the counterpane, instead holding close those feelings of warmth and safety. He made quick work of dressing.

Kitty, he noted, did not protest his impending departure.

"You won't … you won't *tell* anyone, will you?"

"Discretion is at least half the reason my services are so expensive. None will hear of this from me, upon my honor." She gave a dry laugh. "For whatever the honor of a woman like me is worth."

At last, he made himself lift his eyes. "Thank you for your time and company," he said. "I do apologize."

The courtesan gave him a wan smile. "Fortunately, I brought another pair of slippers with me. Good evening, Mr. De Vere."

• • •

When he flung open the door of the little house, it wasn't Rudley Court on a summer's day that greeted him, but the blustery night of an unfamiliar Oxford street.

As he wended his way back to more familiar stomping grounds, the worst of his ordeal slid off his skin to the pavement, from whence he hoped it would be swept up and buried in a dust heap, there to rot into oblivion. But an oily residue of shame remained in his gut, churning and mixing with the discomfort that had plagued him all night, transforming into some acidic poison that trickled into his veins.

What if he wasn't normal? What if he could never truly be with a woman?

Before tonight, Henry's lust had been an unfocused thing he barely comprehended. Women were all big eyes and pouty lips and creamy skin and the impossibly soft, decadent pillows of flesh that plumped over the edges of their bodices. To be sure, he'd heard plenty from the fellows, and he'd pored over dirty pictures like they'd unlock the secrets of the universe, but women—real, flesh-and-blood women—had remained a cypher he couldn't puzzle out, just wanted in the most ferocious, generic way imaginable.

And now that he knew what, precisely, was under those many layers of silks and satins and petticoats, now that he knew what a real woman looked like, felt like, and, God, tasted like—now that he *knew*, his humiliation was all the more shattering. How could he ever bring himself to even approach a woman again? What if this same embarrassment were to befall him?

He was lost in such turbulent thoughts until the lights still blazing in the windows of The Hog's Teeth caught his eye. A dram of something wet and brain-numbing would be most welcome. Ducking into the tavern, he shook droplets of mist from the brim of his hat and clapped his hands before a fire blazing in the huge hearth.

"Henry!" he heard.

Turning, he saw Harrison Dyer at The Honorables' table, waving him over. It seemed ludicrous for them to reserve the large table for themselves now, what with Brandon off in Spain with the Army, Norman living at the Inns of Court in London, and Sheridan flitting about doing whatever it was lazy rich boys did with their days. But Henry and Harrison, younger than the other men and still attending the university, maintained their claim on the table like they were the last survivors of a battle, making their stand.

He plowed through the crowd and took a seat. After catching the attention of the barmaid and ordering a bottle of gin, he started to relax. A frisson of something good and welcome went through his limbs. It wasn't Rudley Court, but in its way, this blasted table was every bit as familiar and safe.

"I wasn't expecting to see you back at our rooms until tomorrow," Harrison said. The caramel-hued eyes of Henry's friend gleamed with interest; a lascivious grin split his face. "What are you doing here? Did you wap her into oblivion, make her plead for a reprieve from the ministrations of your *arbor vitae*? What was it like? What was *she* like?" With the back of his hand, Harrison slapped at Henry's arm. "What were her bubbies like? Use plenty of adjectives."

Henry winced. "You sound like Sheri. I don't want to talk about it." He tipped back a kick of liquor, grimaced at the sharp burn, then poured himself another.

After tossing that one down the hatch and reaching for the gin again, Harrison put a restraining hand on the bottle. "Easy does it, friend o' mine. Sorry if my questions offended. Why the race toward oblivion?"

Propping his elbows on the age-darkened plank of the tabletop, Henry pressed the balls of his hands into his eyes, wishing he could scour the vision of Kitty's horrified expression from his mind. "Something happened," he muttered miserably.

"Did you …" Harrison began in a low voice. "Did you fail to sail the ship into port?"

Henry's head snapped up. Glowering darkly, he poured more of the clear liquor into his glass, then offered the bottle to Harrison. His friend shook his head, pointing out his own mug of cider.

"No trouble at sea," Henry reported. "Good winds, full sail, all that."

Scratching idly at his stubbled chin, Harrison made a thoughtful sound. "Came off too soon?"

Henry hunched over his glass. "No."

"Then what the hell was the problem?"

"I fell asleep," Henry said. "Things got ... queer." Sighing in resignation, he spilled the whole, sordid story.

Making good use of Sheri's birthday gift, Henry had happily rid himself of his virginity with the delectable Kitty. Submitting himself to her tutelage, he'd indulged in hours of bed play and achieved multiple climaxes, each more intense than the last, until, finally, he fell into an exhausted slumber beside his buxom companion. He'd come to abruptly at the sound of Kitty Newman screeching. "Stop! Stop! What are you doing, you disgusting gony? Get away from my slippers! I paid a fortune for those!"

He'd blinked, surprised to see that he was clear across the room from the bed. Had this been his own lodging room, it occurred to Henry that he'd have been in the exact location of his chamber pot. But he wasn't in his room. Instead, he was doing something unspeakable to Kitty Newman's expensive slippers.

"Just a moment," Harrison interrupted. "You took the piss on her shoes?" he tilted his head thoughtfully. "Well that's certainly not the worst thing she must've seen in that profession, chap. In fact, I bet she's gotten any sort of strange request—"

Henry's cheeks flamed. He shook his head emphatically. "I didn't ..." He took a deep, calming breath. "That wasn't it."

Harrison's eyebrows rose, but despite the curiosity on his face, he gave Henry a small, sympathetic smile. The two young men had shared a lodging for some months. In that time, Harrison had retrieved a half-naked Henry from the quadrangle, stopped him from attempting to climb out the window, and prevented several other fiascoes. Harrison always treated Henry's episodes with care and discretion. Even now, he didn't pry for more details than Henry was willing to share.

"I see," he simply said. A lengthy silence fell.

"I'm never going to sleep with a woman again," Henry vowed.

Suddenly, his mind once more returned to Rudley Court. In his mind's eye, Henry saw Claudia Baxter's sweet, guileless face smiling up at him. Her fun-filled schemes never failed to raise his spirits when they were low. A painful yearning pinched his heart.

I want to go home.

Harrison rolled his eyes. "Come on, Hen, it couldn't have been *that* bad."

"It was," Henry insisted, once more hearing Kitty Newman's berating voice ringing in his ears, resurrecting all the night's humiliation. "I mean it, Harry. I will never sleep beside a woman again. I'm broken." A lump formed in his chest. "Who could ever want me?" he challenged his friend. "Who could ever want this?"

Chapter One

The night was stormy, and most certainly dark. And while others might see such weather as portentous of some grave misfortune, to Miss Claudia Baxter, the rain and howling wind were as welcome as a surprise inheritance from a heretofore unheard-of uncle. The appearance of the storm had gifted Claudia an opportunity to deliver herself from a dreadful fate. Not one to ignore such a cosmic boon, she had, over the course of the last two hours, feverishly stitched together an idea.

It was a rather slapdash plan, Claudia allowed, as she padded away from the kitchen with a small bottle of pig's blood gripped in her fist. But with her wedding to Sir Saint Tuggle and his fifty years' worth of dental negligence less than a week off, what choice did she have? At this point, Claudia would have happily run away with a band of Gypsies, had any been so kind as to pass by Rudley Court. Sadly, Roma were thin on the ground in Wiltshire just now, so Claudia was left with a madcap scheme and a vial of blood.

Her bare feet made no sound as she crept through the sleeping house. She and her twin brother, Claude, had discovered—and thereafter avoided—every creaky board and groaning hinge in a childhood spent terrorizing their way through six governesses.

She made her way up to the bedchambers, keeping a keen eye out for Ferguson. The butler's highest calling in life was the preservation of Rudley Court and he'd been known to patrol the halls at least twice per night. In years past, that duty had meant defending the house against the ravages of nine Baxter children, Claudia and Claude being numbers eight and nine.

Luck was with her; Ferguson was nowhere to be seen. Claudia followed the path running down the center of the corridor rug, worn thin by decades of young Baxters and their guests. She stopped outside a guest room door and was startled by a sudden fluttering in her middle. There had been no doubts or fears until this very moment. The little bottle grew slippery in her hand. She passed it to the other and wiped her palm against her dressing gown.

If only her parents hadn't agreed to Sir Saint's proposal, then Claudia wouldn't have been driven to these desperate measures. But she had failed to make a match during her Season. She'd been just another Baxter, with unremarkable looks and an embarrassingly large family. Her two thousand pounds were nothing to brag about, and most of her gowns were handed down from her sisters. Claudia had never been the prettiest, the richest, the most fashionable. And so her Season came and went without a single proposal.

In the five years since, Claudia had resigned herself to the role of spinster aunt to her growing herd of nieces and nephews. Every family needed one, she reasoned. But then, two months ago, disaster struck in the doughy, stinky form of Sir Saint Tuggle. Sir John Baxter had accepted Sir Saint's suit without so much as a by-your-leave from his youngest daughter. Claudia had been informed of her betrothal over the fish course that night.

Sir Saint was due to arrive tomorrow afternoon and stay at Rudley Court until the wedding, and her many siblings would likewise begin trickling in over the course of the week. With the house full of people, Claudia would have no more opportunities to evade this marriage. She was out of time. Unless she took her fate into her own hands, she would become Lady Tuggle in a few days. As her intended had told her, she could look forward to producing Sir Saint's heir, followed by a lifetime of rusticating. There would be no house parties or Seasons in Town or trips abroad. Sir Saint's gout prohibited anything resembling fun from touching his life. She was too young to surrender to such a dreary existence. She couldn't do it. She wouldn't.

Steeling her resolve, Claudia turned the knob.

She slipped into the room and leaned against the beveled wood, allowing her vision to adjust to the darkness of the bedchamber. Outside, the storm still raged. A flash of lightning revealed the bed, as well as a pair of top boots carelessly discarded in the middle of the floor. Plunged once again into darkness, Claudia made her way forward, careful to avoid the boots. One noisy stumble would ruin everything.

With her free hand extended, Claudia reached the bed and felt her way to the top of the covers. A soft exhalation of breath made her heart leap. *It's only Henry*, she reminded herself.

"Only Henry" being Mr. Henry De Vere, whose family's estate, Fairbrook, adjoined the eastern side of Rudley Court. He was twenty-five, two years older than the twins, and had often been about when they were children, tossed in with the Baxters like just another puppy in the litter. Back then, Henry and the twins had been thick as thieves, roaming the countryside and playing games of Claudia's invention. Henry usually sided with her in disputes between the twins and had never let Claude exclude her from their play. Perhaps understandably, she'd developed a touch of hero worship where Henry was concerned. He was her very own champion. As she grew into adolescence, she couldn't help but dream he might come courting some day.

Claude and Henry had gone to Harrow together, and then Henry went off to Oxford. After that ... well, Henry never did come courting. He'd remained a good friend, one she was always happy to see when he visited, but she had long since abandoned fantasies of her next-door neighbor returning the kind of affection she'd carried for him all these years.

Just back from London, Henry had come by earlier today to show off the new horse he'd purchased at Tattersall's. It was the first time Claude and Claudia had seen him in six months. Horse talk had led to tea in the library, which led to an invitation to stay to supper, and then the storm set in and Henry was stuck at Rudley Court for the duration—the unexpected event around which Claudia had hastily formulated her impromptu plan.

Earlier in the evening, when she'd broken the news of her betrothal, Henry's brows had drawn together. "A bit long in the tooth, isn't he?" Henry had asked. Just then, Claudia had wanted to throw her arms around his neck and weep. But the moment passed. He had kissed her cheek and wished her happiness, yet she was sure she'd seen a shadow cross his green eyes.

He would want to help her avoid this marriage, Claudia was certain, even if he didn't approve of her methods. But he would go along with her, as he'd always done.

The long, low mound of his shadow was on the opposite side of the bed. Claudia peeled back the counterpane, revealing the white bottom sheet. She worried at her lower lip while she dithered about what to do. Having seven older siblings meant she was more knowledgeable about particular matters than most young, unmarried ladies. Still, she wasn't entirely certain where to put the blood.

In the regular order of things, the fluid would be beneath her, she decided, in the region of her bottom. She tried to picture where that would be, were she lying on the bed—which she would be, in a moment. That was stage two of The Plan.

She let out a huff of annoyance. This was taking too long. "Bother," she muttered. It would be easier to place herself in the bed first. Then she'd know for sure how to set the scene.

Claudia set down the bottle of blood and untied the sash around her waist. Her dressing gown fell to the floor, leaving her in just her chemise. The decision of what to wear for the occasion of her ruin had caused a moment of consternation, but in the end she decided her usual night rail was too prim for what was meant to look like a night of wanton debauchery.

She crawled onto the bed. The mattress shifted under her weight and Henry's head tossed. Claudia froze, not even daring to breathe. As she knelt there, staring into the darkness with her bottle once again firmly in hand, Claudia realized she could use Henry as a guide.

When she was sure he still slept, Claudia pulled the counterpane back farther, revealing the side of Henry's body.

Henry's *naked* body.

Claudia gulped convulsively. She hadn't reckoned on encountering an unclothed man tonight, no matter what she meant to portray via The Plan.

It didn't matter, she told herself. Henry was asleep and Claudia would soon be—well, maybe not asleep. It would be difficult, knowing she shared the bed with a naked man. But she had to carry on. It was this, or climb into bed with Sir Saint.

Claudia unstoppered the bottle, but then guilt seized her guts, staying her hand. It wasn't just her who would be affected; Henry, too, would be subject to scrutiny. But she remembered the time a dozen years ago, when Henry had taken the blame for breaking Lady Baxter's porcelain fruit bowl, even though it was Claudia who had been pretending it was the hat portion of her regimentals during a battle reenactment in the parlor. He'd thought nothing of subjecting himself to Lady Baxter's ire to save Claudia from punishment.

But perhaps there was a better way. She hadn't explained her predicament to Henry, hadn't enlisted him in her cause. It was one thing to subject herself to her parents' disapprobation; it was another thing entirely to rope Henry into it without his permission.

Henry rolled onto his side just as lightning flashed. For an instant Claudia was blind, but the image of Henry De Vere's body was seared onto the backs of her eyelids. His torso was sculpted with broad shoulders and lean muscle, tapering to a flat stomach and narrow hips. Even relaxed in sleep, the muscles of his chest looked hard beneath a taut covering of skin. Thank heavens, his heavy thigh draped just so, concealing his most private area. Claudia was already stunned by what she'd seen; anything more intimate might cause permanent injury to her nerves. Memory provided a picture of Henry's handsome face: loose waves the color of ripe wheat falling about his ears, high cheekbones and an easy smile, hooded green eyes brimming with laughter. How on earth had she never suspected that familiar face was connected to a body straight off of Lord Elgin's Greek marbles? Probably, she realized, because she'd never given much thought to what a man's body looked like. Henry was beautiful, a word she never thought to apply to a man.

Gradually, Claudia recovered from her shock. She pulled her eyes away from Henry's recumbent form, saw the bed, and gasped. In her stupor, she'd spilled the entire contents of the bottle onto the bed, the stain stark against the white sheets, and growing larger as the fibers wicked the liquid outward from the center of the puddle.

"It's probably worse than it looks," she whispered. No, wait. That wasn't right. Drat Henry De Vere and his mind-muddling physique!

Briefly, she considered waking him. Maybe they could burn the sheets? Then what? When the sun rose, Claudia would still have an unwanted fiancé. No, she decided, better to just follow The Plan. Henry would understand; he would play along.

Claudia restoppered the bottle and shoved it under the bed, then gingerly lay down, keeping well away from the damp mess and the disturbingly alluring man across the bed.

She'd set into motion life-altering events. In the morning, she'd be a ruined woman. Sir Saint would cry off, and Claudia would be saved. Her parents would be furious, of course. Queasiness stole through her as she pictured a look of profound disappointment on her mother's face. But she couldn't allow this wedding to happen. Claudia had made her bed, and now she was lying in it.

She curled up on her side, pulled the counterpane around her ears, and willed everything from her mind but the relentless sounds of the storm.

Chapter Two

Claudia Baxter was in his bed.

He'd dreamed of taking her in the stables, on the sitting room divan, in their childhood treehouse. Once, he'd even dreamed of making love to her while they floated in the river, their entwined bodies buoyed by the gentle current and serenaded by croaking frogs.

This dream was all the sweeter for its simplicity. He was in bed with Claudia beside him, as natural as the beat of his heart. Actually sleeping with her was a fantasy he'd never dared to allow himself before. Her soft hair spilled over the pillow and surrounded her heart-shaped face like a golden-brown halo. Her left arm was flung overhead and her right lay atop her stomach, her fingers curled in a loose fist. There was an adorable little pucker between her brows, as though she dreamed of scolding someone.

He was hard as an oak branch. Her soft warmth invited him over for a cuddle, while her kittenish exhalations made his mouth water for a taste of hers.

Henry scooted into her warm spot and bent his head to her full lips. They were warm and dry. He moistened them with darting laps of his tongue. Claudia's head tilted back, and she sighed.

Oh, yes. Here came Henry's favorite part of his Claudia dreams.

He parted her lips and ran his tongue along the edge of her top teeth. At the same time, he worked his thigh between her legs, laced his fingers with hers, and captured her hands overhead. Satisfaction rumbled deep in his chest. Claudia was warm and pliant beneath him. She tasted sweet and smelled like summer meadows—faintly floral and fresh and so vibrantly *alive.*

Henry deepened the kiss. His tongue swept into her mouth, leisurely exploring. His loins ached with need. The muscles of his stomach twitched. His hips languidly rolled against her, warming up their thrusting motion. That part of the dream was great, too, but Henry tried to prolong the preliminaries.

"Kiss me back, sweet girl," he dream-muttered. "Give me your tongue."

"Why do you want my tongue?" Claudia asked in a husky voice.

Henry lifted his head. A pair of distinctive eyes—soft blue irises ringed with gray—blinked up at him in confusion. His dream-Claudia wasn't usually so bewildered at this point in proceedings.

Wrinkling her nose, Claudia twisted her head to look at their tangled arms. "Will you please release me, Henry? My wrists are twinging." She wrinkled her nose, sniffed. "Henry, I have to tell you something."

His dream-Claudia usually didn't have morning sniffles, either. *Oh, God.* She was awake. He was awake. Claudia Baxter was actually in his bed.

This wasn't such a good dream anymore.

Henry yelped, loud and short. He scrambled back to the other side of the mattress and yanked the counterpane up to cover his … *Oh, my God.* Worse every second. He had actually been on top of Claudia. Naked. And trying to introduce her to his morning constitutional.

Claudia lay as he'd left her, arms overhead, fingers lightly tangled in her hair. Anxiety clouded her eyes. They darted toward the door—

Which opened. "Everything all right, Henry?"

Claude Baxter, Henry's friend since childhood and the twin brother of the woman in his sheets, stepped into the room and froze. Only his eyes, grayer than Claudia's, moved, darting between the occupants of the bed.

"Claude," Henry started. "This isn't what it …" Language abandoned him. He had no idea what this was. Why was Claudia in his bed? Henry only had a few drinks with Claude after supper last night, not enough to bed a woman and forget about it.

Just then, a low snort emerged from Claude. His eyes narrowed on Henry and his head dropped, like a bull about to charge. Henry had no doubt that he was the red cape.

"I'm going to kill you," Claude ground out between clenched … everything. His jaw was locked and his lips pulled back in a snarl. The cords on his neck stood out like … something very prominent. It was too early in the morning to deal in metaphor.

"You *bastard*," Claude spat. "How could you?"

Claudia propped up on her elbows. Wisps of light brown hair tangled around her shoulders and biceps. Her lips, plumped by his kiss, pushed out in a pout. She wore a thin chemise, through which Henry could detect the lines of her breasts and the dusky shadows of her nipples. She looked precisely like she'd been tumbled. "Stop shouting, Claude! You're giving me the headache." She scratched the side of her nose and plopped back into the pillows.

"Claude, get out of that bed," her brother demanded.

"Go awaaay," Claudia moaned. "I didn't sleep well last night."

Henry dropped his face into his hands. "Not helping, Claudia."

"What on earth is all the commo—*gah*!"

Lady Baxter, the plump mother hen of her gaggle, had been a second mama to Henry. Over the years, she'd welcomed him into her home countless times and treated him as one of her own little chicks. And now she stood in the doorway of his guest room, hands pressed to her cheeks.

Claude stomped across the room and yanked open the curtains, just in time to illuminate Sir John Baxter's arrival on the scene. The baronet's wheeze of dismay sucked all the air out of the room. "Henry De Vere!" the twins' father bellowed. "What is the meaning of this infamy?"

Henry's underarms went clammy. He shifted his posture, trying to find a position to restore a modicum of his dignity. He quickly deduced there was not one. "Sir, I don't know what to say." Henry raked a hand through his hair. "I didn't … That is to say, Claudia and I, we did not …"

Beside him, Claudia lay there like a lump, staring at the ceiling. "Sit up," he hissed. "Tell them nothing happened."

With obvious reluctance, Claudia dragged herself to a sitting position, eyes downcast and bare shoulders hunched. *Say something*, he silently begged.

Lady Baxter gasped. "Claudia Baxter, cover yourself!"

The young woman's cheeks turned pink. Despite his own shock and dismay, a pang of sympathy shot through Henry. Whatever had happened, Claudia didn't deserve this humiliation.

He secured the covers between his arms and sides and lifted his hands, palms out. "Let's calm ourselves, please, and discuss this in a rational fashion." When the impending riot seemed to have quelled, Henry gestured to the woman beside him. "Miss Baxter, there seems to have been some misunderstanding. If you would be so good as to enlighten us, I'm sure we'll all be glad to put this mystery behind us."

From behind the curtain of her hair, Claudia sent him an apologetic look. Then she drew a breath, squared her shoulders, and slid from the bed. She bent over, giving Henry a glimpse of her lush backside. He covered a strangled sound with a cough. When he looked again, Claudia had wrapped up in a dressing gown.

"Now," he said, "please tell us what happened. Which was nothing," he added for the benefit of the other three Baxters in his room, his voice rising in righteous indignation. "Absolutely nothing …"

Fwump went the counterpane as Claudia pulled it back with a flourish, revealing a startling patch of crimson, ominous and large.

"… happened."

• • •

It hadn't quite sunk in for them yet, but Claudia had won. While Mama and Papa and Claude and Henry all stared at the evidence on the sheet, their minds would be busy adding one and one and subtracting Sir Saint from the equation. She was safe now. She wouldn't have to marry that gouty toad and spend nights in his bed. Even though she hadn't yet had an opportunity to explain things to Henry, the freedom of release expressed itself in an irrepressible grin she shared with her nearest and dearest. *Isn't it wonderful*, she wanted to crow.

Oh, the others were still absorbing the sight and what it confirmed—or, what they thought it confirmed, anyway—which was more than enough confirmation to send even the most ardent lover on a quest to rip down the banns. Once he caught wind of this, Sir Saint, who was nothing approaching an ardent lover, would waddle his rotund self away from Rudley Court and out of her life forever. Unexpectedly, her eyes filled with tears of relief as the crushing dread of her impending marriage fell away.

Claude seemed to recover from the shock first. "Forgive me for posing an indelicate question, Mother, but is that a normal … quantity?"

Lady Baxter's hands were fisted below her eyes, as though she could scarcely bring herself to look at the sheets. At Claude's question, she shook her head. "That's more blood than I saw all eight times I was brought to childbed, including for you twins." Her face crumpled and she rounded on Henry. "What did you *do* to her?"

Claudia glanced at the bed. Now that she saw her work in the light of day, there did seem to be a shocking quantity of blood. The bottle was so small, though; it had contained scarcely enough liquid to fill a teacup. Was that really too much? She didn't know— she was a virgin, for mercy's sake!

Henry was as stunned as everyone else, of course. "I would never do anything to Miss Baxter to result in this …"

His face took on a green cast. Oh, no! He couldn't get sick. That would distract everyone from arriving at the moral of the story, which was *Claudia cannot marry Sir Saint, she is ruined. Ruined for matrimony. Ruined forever.*

"It looks like a slaughterhouse," Sir John contributed. His face had gone nearly as dark as the impressive stain. His wife was buried against his shoulder, looking away from the scene of their daughter's transgression. Her keening wail rose in the air.

"You're going to die," Claude said, his words icily clipped.

"No, I'm not," Claudia said. "Did you not know virgins spill some blood on their—"

The inhuman roar that burst from her twin's throat was a tad unsettling.

"Not helping, Claudia," Henry said for the second time.

Her arms crossed at her waist, Claudia shot Henry an annoyed glance. The greenish cast to his face had given way to a waxy pallor. "Hush and let me handle this," she instructed him.

"Name your second," Claude growled. He hadn't finished dressing before bursting into Henry's room, Claudia noted. The open neck of his shirt showed skin flushed with fury. "Name your weapon. Write your will and sign it in blood, because you die tomorrow morning, De Vere."

Claudia's mouth dropped as Claude's words struck home. "You meant *Henry* was going to die, not me?"

"Of course not you, peabrain," her brother snapped. "Your honor has been impugned, or haven't you noticed?"

"Well, you aren't fighting a duel," she proclaimed. A duel! How positively fustian. All she wanted was to not have the wedding of her nightmares. "Papa, tell Claude he isn't going to shoot Henry."

Sir John looked like he'd happily chuck the lot of them into the abyss. His mouth opened, but her brother butted in yet again, the mannerless lout.

"I demand satisfaction!"

Claudia's fists dug into her hips. "And *I* demand you stop this nonsense *at once*!" If there was a human being she felt completely at ease screeching at, it was her twin. And screech she did. How dare he threaten Henry? "Mr. De Vere has been your best friend for twenty years, and at the first provocation, you're ready to do murder?" She was enjoying her impromptu role of Defender of the Wrongly Accused. Her eyes, she was sure, blazed with the light of Justice. "I'm ashamed to call you my brother, and weep that we ever shared a womb. I should rather be cast into the wilderness, penniless and alone, than admit connection to a bloodthirsty turncoat such as your foul self."

Claude hadn't heard a word of her monologue, which was fair enough, she supposed, given she'd not paid attention to the harangue he'd simultaneously delivered. The volume of their argument filled the room—and probably the entire house.

A tug at her waist brought Claudia back down onto the edge of the bed. "That's enough now." Henry's rich voice was velvet against her ear, while Claude's continued rant was the roughest burlap. Briefly, she met Henry's eyes. His olive-green gaze spoke of steady resolve. Claudia felt a melting sensation in her chest.

"Claude," Henry said, raising his voice.

Her brother's lips pinched together. His chin continued to work back and forth, as though his angry words were fighting to break past the barrier of his teeth.

Henry rearranged the covers tucked around his torso. He looked at the bloody bed and then back to Claude. "If you insist, of course I'll meet you. I'd rather not duel my friend, but I understand. However, I want you—all of you"—he glanced at Sir John and Lady Baxter—"to know that Claudia and I will be married at once."

The bed seemed to tilt beneath Claudia's rump. Marry Henry? That wasn't how she'd envisioned him going along with the pretense of her ruin. This had all gone wrong. "No," she blurted. "Henry, I can't marry you. You don't understand—"

Henry's mouth twitched downward. "You *must* marry me, Claudia. After this …" He gestured to the mess. A shiver shook his shoulders. "I'll leave for London at once and procure a special license. As soon as I'm back, we'll marry."

"The hell you will!" cut in a new voice.

Claudia's gaze jerked to the door, where her parents shuffled aside to make room for Sir Saint Tuggle. Behind him, Ferguson, the butler, wrung his hands and issued abject apologies to Sir John, which were ignored.

"What are you doing here?" Claudia blurted. This fiasco just kept picking up momentum. "You're not supposed to be here until this afternoon!"

Her fiancé's prodigious nose sniffed. His ample lower lip drooped in a wet moue of distaste. One plump hand smoothed the blue fabric of his coat, while the other gripped the ivory handle of a walking stick. He tottered into the room on swollen, stockinged feet stuffed into black slippers. At the other end, a curled white wig perched atop his head.

"Can you blame a fellow for being eager to see his bride, what? I was settling into my guest chamber, heard shouting, and came to see what all the commotion was about." Sir Saint lifted his walking stick and jabbed it threateningly at Henry. "I don't know what you're up to, you jackanapes, but you will desist at once. Miss Baxter is marrying me."

Chapter Three

As Sir John led away a fuming Sir Saint, soon followed by Lady Baxter shepherding out her daughter, a single thought lay heavy on Henry's mind:

Perhaps I did it.

Claude still tramped about the room, chest heaving like a bellows. "Damn it, Henry! Why? Why Claudia? Of all the sisters in the world, why did you do this to *mine*? Why not Schneiderman's sister? He deserves it, after pissing on your cat that time."

Henry's gaze slid to the linens-cum-murder scene. "I don't remember doing this, Claude, I swear."

His friend dragged a hand through his brown hair and scoffed. "Don't remember? If you think that's going to stop me from putting one right between your eyes, you're—oh. *Oh.*" His startled gray eyes widened. "In your sleep? But you haven't done anything funny in a long time."

Henry groaned. "I know. But what else could it have been?"

As a child, Henry was a terrible sleepwalker. Every night, he rose from his bed and wandered. Sometimes he remained within the confines of the nursery. Other times, he awoke elsewhere in the house. Once, he woke up as Cook snatched a handful of cookies away from him. He'd already eaten a dozen, and was plowing his way through a dozen more when she'd found him. In another incident, he'd come to in the garden, shivering on frosty grass.

A doctor summoned from London had diagnosed Henry with somnambulism, and assured his parents he'd eventually outgrow the condition. For years, this was not the case. When he stayed the night with the Baxters, he walked in his sleep. When he went to Harrow, he walked in his sleep. Thankfully, he'd shared a dormitory room with Claude, who was long-used to his condition.

Every night, Claude locked the door and hid the key, so Henry couldn't wander the grounds. He'd sometimes pull books from shelves or scribble nonsense on foolscap, but the other boys had never learned his secret, and Claude had never teased him for it.

University presented another challenge. Once, Henry had gained consciousness outside The Hog's Teeth, half a mile from his lodging. Thankfully, Harrison had found him before he actually entered the establishment in his nightshirt. A moment later, the other Honorables arrived on the scene. The four men had shielded Henry from prying eyes as they escorted him home. The truth then came out, but none of the men had mocked him—not even Sheri, whose native tongue was derision. That night, Harrison stayed with Henry, and the two lodged together for the remainder of their time at Oxford.

Over time, Henry's nocturnal activities occurred with less frequency, until finally, about four years ago, they stopped.

Or so he thought.

"If this happened in my sleep," Henry said, gesturing to the brownish-red sheet that had become the most important scrap of fabric ever to feature in his life, "why would Claudia be here, in my room, instead of I in hers?"

Claude thumped his fists against his temples. "Ugh! Stop making me think about my sister like this. I don't know! During your noctambulation, you must have absconded with her, brought her back here, and raped her."

There it was, the knife to his gut. The word no one had been willing to say, even though they were all thinking it. It was the only explanation for the sheer quantity of blood. Someone had hurt Claudia, badly.

It must have been him.

"No," he protested. "No. I wouldn't. I wouldn't."

The thought of anyone hurting Claudia—sweet, funny, harebrained Claudia—made him feel homicidal. The notion that *he* was the villain … It just wasn't possible. He would die before harming her. Even asleep, he wouldn't do it.

Henry's elbows dug into his sheet-covered thighs; he shook his head against his clasped hands, as though pleading for deliverance. "Something about this isn't right."

His friend's head cocked to the side. "Really? And what was your first clue? Was it my ravished sister in your bed, or the pint of blood on the linens?"

Snapping his head up, Henry scowled. "Not that, arse-for-brains. But Claudia didn't seem as upset as you'd think, given the circumstances, did she?"

"She was deranged from blood loss, most like."

Henry made a rude gesture. He closed his eyes and tried to ignore Claude's knuckle rapping against the window. Maybe Claudia had been in shock, he allowed, but she hadn't protested when she'd awoken with a naked man atop her body, kissing her. Henry pushed aside the fleeting memory of soft lips and satin skin. And then she'd matter-of-factly told her brother what was what when it came to the loss of one's virginity. Claudia hadn't really reacted adversely to anything, until Henry declared they would marry.

"I suppose I've made trouble for Claudia and Sir Saint," he said, sparing a thought for the man. "I hope he doesn't treat her badly for this."

Claude snorted. "He just found his fiancée in bed with another man. Of course he's going to treat her badly. Not *too* badly, I hope," Claude said, raising a finger. "I've already got you to kill tomorrow. I don't want to overtax my schedule."

"Maybe he'll cry off," Henry said with a wisp of hope. "He must."

He recalled the acid burning its way up his throat when Claudia had given him the news of her betrothal yesterday evening. Henry's brother, Duncan, had shared the news with him in a letter dated a week ago, but Henry couldn't believe it. Surely, his brother had the wrong of it. Sir Saint Tuggle was a miserable old lech, and Henry couldn't imagine the girl he'd secretly carried a torch for all these years allowing herself to be forced into such a distasteful match.

There was plenty of work at De Vere and Sons's London offices to keep him busy, but Henry'd had to come home and hear it from Claudia herself. Even when she'd said the words, he didn't want to believe it. The sadness in her soft blue eyes was what had finally convinced him she was telling the truth. Claudia had never been able to lie to him with a straight face.

No one else had offered for her, and she couldn't go on living at Rudley Court forever, he realized. Sir John was every bit of seventy, and Lady Baxter was sixty-and-some. They had to make sure their youngest daughter was provided for while they were still here to do so. She needed a husband. And so he had grasped her hands and kissed her soft cheek, the way a dutiful friend should, all the while selfishly wanting to beg her not to go through with it.

"You do see that she and I must marry," Henry blurted.

His friend shot him an incredulous look. "Is that why you did this? So you could have Claudia for yourself?"

"Christ, no!" he evaded. There was no socially acceptable way to inform one's friend you had lusted after his sister for some number of years. Besides, when he'd vowed never to slumber beside another woman, he had sworn off any possibility of marriage, as well. He'd accepted that he and Claudia could never be more than friends, because he couldn't bear that she might some day look upon him with the kind of disgust Kitty Newman had that long-ago night.

Henry slapped his open hand against his chest. "You know I never meant to marry. It wouldn't be fair to subject a woman to … this." He gestured down the length of his body, coughing a bitter laugh. "But now there's no choice. Claudia could be—" His throat seized.

"Could be breeding," Claude finished. He planted his hands on his hips and exhaled a heavy sigh. "That might be a problem, me killing you, if it turns out Claudia's in the family way. Although, I suppose she could still marry Tuggle, and he can raise your by-blow."

As if Henry would ever allow that to happen! He remembered how she'd looked and felt this morning, delectably rumpled, and imagined her in bed with Sir Saint, instead of him. The homicidal rage he'd felt earlier narrowed in focus. The additional possibility of his own child landing in the clutches of another man brought out instincts Henry didn't know he possessed. Some primordial urge to defend and protect his own tightened his chest. His nostrils flared.

"She might not have been mine yesterday, but Claudia is damned well mine today," he snapped. "And you will not mention a duel again, Claude, do you understand? Duels are for bored aristocrats who call each other out over who owns more game birds." He rose and faced the other man across the bed. Sweeping his arms wide, Henry declared, "I'm prepared to take full responsibility for something I don't even remember doing, so kindly desist with that line of talk." He jabbed a finger toward Claude. "We are going to be brothers, so you may as well make your peace with it now."

Claude's lip curled. "For God's sake, man, put on some clothes."

And with that, he walked out, leaving Henry alone with his fired-up emotions.

If Sir Saint thought he was going to steal Claudia back, he was destined for bitter disappointment. The sooner Henry sent Tuggle packing, the sooner he could get on with marrying the girl he'd had no thought of marrying until half an hour ago.

Chapter Four

Claudia was bundled into her room and left to dress while her mother and Mrs. Johnson, the housekeeper, carried out a hushed conversation in the corridor. Like so much of her wardrobe, the ecru morning dress Claudia pulled on had belonged to an older sister—Jillian, probably, although it might have been Maggie. She fingered a darned spot at the waist. Given the condition of the fabric, it very well may have gone through both of the next-oldest girls.

All things considered, the morning hadn't gone *too* badly, Claudia decided. The Plan had been a success in execution and immediate outcome: She was ruined. It was the unforeseen effects that had her worried, namely Sir Saint appearing on the scene and declaring he was still marrying her. Didn't the foolish man realize what had happened? Claudia was incensed that her fiancé didn't seem to be taking her status as a fallen woman very seriously.

Her parents were anxious and angry and hurt. She'd known they would be, but witnessing her mother's white-lipped dismay had made Claudia feel like the lowliest worm. If there was a way to put Mama's mind at ease, she'd do so in a heartbeat. But successfully avoiding marriage to Sir Saint meant keeping up the appearance of ruination. *Poor Claude*, she mused, recalling her twin's fury. She hoped he'd calmed down by now. It certainly wouldn't do to have him bring on an apoplexy through his overdeveloped sense of fraternal duty. What the rest of the Baxter clan would think of Claudia, once this scandal worked its way through the familial vines of communication, didn't bear contemplating.

Her shoulders tensed as a feeling of dread swept through her. Perhaps this hadn't been the wisest course of action. But there simply hadn't been time to think of anything better, and now that she'd done it, she had to see this thing through.

And as for Henry … Now that she'd had a little time to think about it, his "proposal" was probably the best idea he could come up with on the spur, given they'd not had a chance to plan what he would say when they were discovered. It was very clever of him to catch on to the situation so quickly and devise a script, even if it was a touch too far. Now, she'd have to try to think of a reason to tell her parents why she wouldn't be marrying either Henry or Sir Saint.

Recalling Henry's statement that they would marry, pronounced in such a calm, factual manner, made her heart give a funny little hop. There was a time when she'd dreamed of receiving a declaration from him. In all the years she'd known him, though, he'd never shown anything but friendly interest in Claudia. And so she must content herself with hearing a faux proposal and remaining his friend.

Just a friend? said some little devil inside her head. *Remember when you woke up with a very naked Henry atop you and you did nothing to encourage his relocation? Quite the friend you are.*

Mrs. Baxter let herself back into the room. "My dear," she started, "you should be in bed! I've sent for the surgeon." Her hands crossed her middle and gripped her waist. "Do you think Mr. Whombleby will suffice? I can send for the midwife, if you'd prefer."

It was on the tip of Claudia's tongue to ask why the village surgeon had been summoned, but she stopped herself. Perhaps it was usual to undergo an examination after losing one's virginity. The incident did seem to inspire a great deal of concern over her welfare. She supposed one's husband would be the person to request the surgeon's attendance, in the customary way of things. Still, it seemed an awful lot of fuss.

And what if Mr. Whombleby discovered her fraud? The idea that she might somehow be un-ruined sent a thrill of dread down her back. "Is that necessary? I'm quite well."

Her mother's chin quivered; tears welled in her gray eyes. She brought her hands to Claudia's cheeks. "My darling girl. I know it's difficult, but you must be brave. I shall be right here with you. I won't leave you for a moment. He might …" Her voice caught. She cleared her throat. "Mr. Whombleby might have to perform an examination, to ascertain what's happened."

Claudia let out a nervous laugh. She stepped to her vanity and plucked at a ribbon on the table. "Doesn't he see this sort of thing quite a bit?" She imagined June, in particular, must be a busy month for the surgeon, calling on new brides the morning after the wedding.

"I should hope not!"

"Well, I wouldn't think an examination necessary. I don't suppose I'm a special case." She flashed a smile, as though to prove her health. "The pertinent thing is that my wedding cannot take place," she pointed out, since no one had bothered to arrive at this conclusion.

Her mother let a long breath through her nostrils. "You needn't fret about that, dear. Your father and Sir Saint are still in the study." A worried frown deepened the pleats between her brows. "Your father will set it all to rights, love, I promise. He will make sure your wedding proceeds as planned."

The thought of Sir Saint—whose mother must have been the most optimistic woman in Christendom when she dubbed her progeny thusly—doing anything other than demanding to be released of the betrothal set Claudia's nerves aflame. "No!" she insisted. "I cannot marry Sir Saint now, not for all the world. Henry ruined me."

There was a knock at the door, three firm raps. When she opened it, Henry stood on the other side. The eyes that met hers had a haunted look about them. His green irises had darkened to the color of damp moss. Fine lines creased the skin around them. He was in pain, Claudia realized with a start. It rolled off of him and into her, until her fingers trembled and her heart squeezed so hard she feared it would turn inside out. What on earth?

Over her shoulder, Lady Baxter clucked her tongue, breaking their silent connection. "Shoo, Henry! You cannot be in Claudia's bedchamber."

"Forgive my intrusion, but I wondered if I might beg a few moments of Miss Baxter's time?" He spoke carefully, formally, in a manner at odds with his place in the household. He fretted with his left sleeve; Claudia noticed it was not closed with a cufflink, as the other sleeve was.

"Of course," Claudia said, at the same instant Lady Baxter squawked, "Absolutely not!"

Henry's lips drew into a line, straight as a blade. "Lady Baxter, I know I've no right to request privacy with Claudia, but I must insist. I *cannot* leave this house without speaking to her." He took a single, small step; his toes crossed the threshold.

Warmth touched Claudia's cheek—his warmth. A scant foot of space separated them. She had to resist the compulsion to retreat. Heavens, when had he grown so large? Her physical awareness of the man had taken on a keener edge. His wide shoulders quite filled the doorway. It would take a battering ram to budge past him, if he put his mind to staying there.

The sight of him, so grim and determined, cast Henry in a new light. It was as though she'd never seen him before. Even last night, when she'd encountered him without clothes, he was the same Henry she'd always known—relaxed, approachable … albeit slightly more prone to taking a chill. But this man, dressed in the same buckskin riding breeches and maroon cutaway coat he'd worn yesterday, was an unknown. If she didn't know he had no twin, she might think she stood in the presence of Henry's identical sibling.

"Perhaps a walk?" she suggested.

"Out of the question!" Lady Baxter's fierce scowl showed she was not impressed by Henry's persistence. "I wouldn't leave you alone with a dog, to say nothing of Claudia. If it weren't for my friendship with your dear mother, I would have you before the magistrate." The ruffle of her white cap quivered with the force of her maternal ire. "It still may happen, if Sir Saint will not have Claudia. Such a scandal it would cause, to say nothing of poor Judith's nerves. If your mother succumbs from the indignity of this, Henry, it shall be on your head."

Henry snorted as he shouldered his way past Claudia and Lady Baxter. "If scandal is inevitable, then a conversation with my intended can't make it any worse. And if you've decided to hush this all up, then no harm will be done."

Claudia gasped. "I'm not your intended," she protested.

Hands planted on hips, Henry leveled a stern look at her. "We need to talk, Claudia."

With a huff, she relented. Obviously, they did need to talk, since he was carrying on with this charade of proposing to her. "I think he's right, Mama," she said. "We'll just step onto the terrace. You can watch us from the door."

"Fine," snapped Lady Baxter. "Just see if I don't."

She herded the young people through the house to a parlor. Lady Baxter wove through sofas and chairs numerous enough to seat the Baxter hordes, then flung wide the French window opening onto the terrace overlooking the garden. The beds and rows of plantings carried the same thready, overused air as the house. A gloomy morning threatened to resume the prior night's rain.

"Against my better judgment," Lady Baxter said, casting a disapproving look first at Henry, and then Claudia, "you may have ten minutes. Dear, I shall let you know if Mr. Whombleby arrives."

The window closed and Henry rounded on Claudia. The haunted look in his eyes was back. The planes of his cheekbones underscored his anxiety. "Why Mr. Whombleby? Claudia, are you …? God, did I truly hurt you?"

As threatened, Lady Baxter stood at the door, the tip of her nose touching the glass, her wide eyes trained on Claudia and Henry. It was rather unnerving.

Claudia's tongue swept over her lips. Prickly sweat erupted on her palms. "Of course you didn't hurt me, Henry," she said sotto voce.

He pinched the bridge of his nose. A wave of dark gold hair flopped onto his forehead. "Don't lie to me, please. Spare me nothing."

She was truly befuddled by this performance. If anyone knew the truth, it was Henry! Why was he attempting to keep his part of the ruse going? He didn't seem to be going about it in a very convincing manner. Claudia thought bedding women was something of a hobby for much of the male population, but poor Henry was going on as though it was tragic.

Maybe … A thought began to take shape. Maybe Henry didn't know how to act because he lacked experience, too. She laid a reassuring hand on his arm. A sharp rap on the glass had her jerking her hand back to her side.

Henry turned to the balustrade. His long fingers curled, claw-like, around the stone. The fine summer wool of his coat strained across the back as his shoulders hunched.

"It's the normal visit from the surgeon," she assured him, careful of her words. She knew from experience that sound carried through the glass of the French windows. She couldn't speak too plainly, for fear of revealing the deception to her mother.

His silence took on an angry pulse.

"Normal for this situation," she continued, wary now. He was furious at her. In the past, he'd never treated her with anything more negative than occasional indifference. Over the years, he'd humored her playroom dictates, laughed at her hoydenish antics, smiled fondly when they danced at her debut ball. She'd always been so sure of his regard, her dear, reliable Henry. She'd taken him for granted, assumed he'd be happy in his willingness to go along with The Plan, failed to imagine him capable of hating her. "Mother says it's necessary," she finished miserably.

Shudders wracked Henry's body. How he must despise her now! Tears pricked the backs of her eyes. "I'm sorry," she murmured. "So sorry. I wish you wouldn't be angry with me, Henry. I understand, but I hate it. If only I could take it back!"

He whipped around. "Angry at you? Oh, my God, how could I—?" Hands shaking, he reached for her shoulders. Another warning tap on the glass. Henry ignored it. His fingers curled around her arms with exquisite care, handling her as though she were as fragile as a moth's wing. "How could I ever be angry at you?" His hooded eyes swam with sorrow. "I hate myself for what I've done to you, Claudia. If you'd rather marry Sir Saint, I wouldn't blame you. But I'm responsible, and so ..." On the inside, Claudia was flattened by the raw anguish she saw in his face. "I swear, I will spend the rest of my life trying to make this right."

Rough fingertips skimmed down her arms. He took her hands and, with delicate tenderness, raised them to his lips. Each was anointed with a reverent kiss. A pleasurable ache settled in the pit of her stomach. Lady Baxter's rapping at the door threatened to shatter the glass.

"Please," Henry said. "Please say you'll marry me."

Henry had never been any good during the annual Baxter family Christmas play. But he was game for just about anything and always allowed Claudia to rope him into her productions. She once gave him the coveted part of the angel speaking to the shepherds. Rather than Good Tidings of Great Joy, Henry delivered his lines like a particularly menacing rendition of the Riot Act. After that, she'd relegated him to the role of Rapt Bystander, a nonspeaking character she'd devised just for him. He'd never managed to carry off a convincing version of rapt, either.

Suffice it to say, Henry wasn't pretending anything. He was sincerely proposing marriage to her, and he was so sad about it. She wanted to throw her arms around his neck and comfort him. She wanted to burst into tears. This was wrong. All wrong.

The French window slammed open. "Hands off!" Lady Baxter barked. "Claudia, return to your room at once. Mr. Whombleby will be here any moment."

Henry's eyes never left hers. His pleading, anguished eyes.

She couldn't let him do this. There was no need for him to throw himself onto the sacrificial altar of matrimony for the sake of her ruse. "No," she said, her voice pitched low. "You've misunderstood everything. It's all right, Henry, you don't have to marry me. You ... we won't. We won't."

His face went strangely blank as Lady Baxter grabbed Claudia's wrist and tugged her into the house.

• • •

Well.

That was horrible.

A fresh wave of guilt ripped through Henry. He braced his arms against the balustrade and took deep breaths, pushing down the competing urges to rage and weep and vomit. The lush scent of honeysuckle, blanketing a nearby arched trellis, helped calm him.

Two decades of friendship with Claudia, gone, thanks to the machinations of his sleeping mind. In another life, they could have made a go of it. If circumstance had somehow drafted them into marriage, Henry believed they would have found happiness.

Claudia would have made a face at him while they stood at the altar. He'd have struggled to retain composure in front of their families, but probably would have laughed anyway, right in the face of God and the vicar. And together, smiling, they'd have found a way to turn their friendship into something more.

Deep breaths became shallow pants as he stared blindly over the garden. All he could see was Claudia, beautiful and hurting as she refused him. He should be grateful she'd spoken to him at all, and not slammed the door in his face. And now she had to be attended by the surgeon—the surgeon! His mouth tasted of ashes.

Behind him, there was a clearing of a throat.

The butler, Ferguson, stood just inside the parlor. "Your horse has been saddled and brought around, Mr. De Vere." Agitated fingers twitched at his sides. The old retainer was clearly distressed by having to evict a family friend of long-standing.

He might not have been a military man, but Henry knew a strategic retreat was in order. He straightened, noting how unbalanced his arms felt. When he'd hastily dressed, he'd been unable to locate both of his cufflinks. Odd how the weight of such a small thing could make a difference in his equanimity. Mustering his composure, he acknowledged the butler with a detached smile. "Thank you, Ferguson."

The Baxters could kick him out of Rudley Court, but they couldn't keep him away from Claudia forever. Whatever it took, he had to earn her forgiveness and convince her to marry him. And with Claudia due to marry Tuggle in less than a week, he couldn't afford to stay away from her for even a day.

As he swung up onto his horse, Henry plotted.

Chapter Five

An hour ago, hauling a ladder from Fairbrook's gardening shed through the woods to Rudley Court in the dead of night had seemed a good idea. But that had been two miles, one turned ankle, and three slivers in his palm ago.

The weak light of a quarter moon did not penetrate the early summer canopy topping the coombe marking the border between the estates, and so there was a great deal of stumbling and cursing involved in Henry's quest. Maneuvering the tall ladder across the ancient-wooded inclines had been a painstaking task. When, at last, he topped the ravine between Rudley Court and Fairbrook, Henry dropped the ladder to catch his breath.

It was at that moment he realized he almost certainly could have found a ladder somewhere about Rudley Court, and saved himself the strain of lugging this one all over Creation. "Curse me for a dim-witted ass."

Hands braced on knees, back aching, and shoulders burning, Henry reflected on the events that had brought him to this juncture in time. Other than thinking to burgle Sir John's gardening equipment instead of his own, he wasn't sure if changing any part of his past would have averted the current crisis. Henry couldn't help his sleepwalking any more than he could stop himself from being attracted to Claudia.

That knowledge didn't prevent another pang of guilt from thudding painfully through his chest. If he'd been more cautious, if he hadn't allowed himself to be lulled into thinking his sleepwalking days were behind him, this wouldn't have happened. But why *had* it happened? After years of remaining in his bed at night, why had Henry suddenly done something far worse than he ever had back in university, when his somnambulism had been most trying?

When he went to Oxford, he'd thought *surely* his condition was behind him, as though somnambulism itself was an entity who had received notice of Henry's completion of studies at Harrow and took that as his cue to enjoy his pension in a little cottage in the country, perhaps spending his days puttering about the garden, or raising goats. But no, the bastard followed Henry to university. And though his bouts of sleepwalking became less frequent as he entered young manhood, the degree of horror to which he was subjected upon waking increased. To this day, Henry couldn't think the name Kitty Newman without fleetingly wishing for a swift, merciful death.

Of course, the promised moment Henry had spent years longing for, the day when he outgrew his somnambulism, came and went without notice. It was only in retrospect that Henry realized he'd finally outlasted his nocturnal nemesis. One day, it occurred to him that it had been a month since Harrison had prevented Henry from burning down the boarding house by trying to light a pipe in his sleep. He seemed to hold his breath every night thereafter, wondering, as he readied himself for bed, if his good fortune would hold. It did. Gradually, as weeks and months passed without further incident, Henry had relaxed. The nightmare was over.

Except, it wasn't.

His sleepwalking had returned, and Henry would chain himself to his own bed every night if that's what it took to prevent him from ever again doing anything such as happened last night. He'd created this damnable mess with Claudia; he'd bloody well fix it, too.

"Almost there," he said, rallying himself with a fresh wave of determination.

Then he hauled up the unwieldy ladder, hooked his arm through, and balanced the rail on his shoulder. Cognizant of the earth's appointment with dawn in about four hours, Henry set off at a lope. He managed to maintain that light running pace through the bleaching green behind the stables.

He was breathless once more when, at last, he rounded the southeastern corner of the house and came to a stop below Claudia's second-story window.

The ladder rasped over the bricks as he moved it into place. It reached to a couple feet below the windowsill. Perfect.

After an easy ascent, Henry faced his own dim reflection in the pane. He cupped one hand against the glass and peered in. Claudia's fire had burned down; the embers gave a feeble glow, not enough for him to make out much of the interior.

Henry tapped on the glass. No response. A breeze tickled the back of his neck and gave him the slightest bit of vertigo. He glanced at the ground twenty feet below, gulped, squeezed his eyes, and tapped again.

Nothing.

The next time, Henry knocked in earnest, as if he was standing at the door rather than precariously perched outside the window.

He detected motion in the bed. Claudia rolled over the edge of the mattress. Her hands tangled in the sheets, stopping her from collapsing to the floor. She staggered over and climbed onto the window seat, fumbled with the latch, and drew the window inward.

Strands of hair had come loose from her braid and tangled about her neck. Her eyes squinted; her nose scrunched like a bunny's. "Henry?" she said, her voice husky with sleep. "Is that you?"

She stood on her knees, putting their faces level with one another. She blinked and rubbed her eyes with a fist.

"May I come in?" he asked.

She giggled. "Henry, what are you doing? You're floating outside my window!"

"I'm not …" He took in the silly smile and the dazed, glassy sheen of her eyes. She was barely awake. "Will you please move aside so I can come in?"

Just then, Claudia lurched forward and flung her arms around Henry's neck. For a terrifying instant, he felt the weightless, dizzying sensation of backward motion as the ladder teetered away from the house.

"I'm so glad you're here!" she exclaimed.

Henry grasped the windowsill so tightly, pain throbbed through his knuckles. "Claudia," he grunted, "back away. Slowly."

She shot him a confused frown, but did as he asked, scrambling down from the window seat and holding her hands against her chest.

He allowed himself a minute to take several calming breaths and hazard a guess as to how many gray hairs he'd just sprouted. Then he bent his knees and neatly vaulted over the sill. His long legs cleared the seat; his feet came to rest on the other side.

The young woman gaped. "Gracious, wherever did you learn to float like that?"

He scowled. What was wrong with her? Even at her silliest, Claudia wasn't this goosebrained. "I climbed a ladder, like any ordinary man sneaking into the rooms of a young lady in the middle of the night would do."

She giggled again and sauntered toward him, her hips loosely swaying inside her white night rail. She walked two fingers up his chest and throat. Henry gulped. The digits rounded his chin and forded his lips. Her touch was soft, like the pattering of a kitten. A heavy coil of wanting unfurled in his midsection and rolled through his groin and down the backs of his legs.

"You. Are. So. Funny," she said, accentuating each word with a tap on the end of his nose. Her lips looked unbearably inviting.

Somehow, his hands found their way to her waist. He stroked up and down, from the base of her ribcage to the tops of her hips.

With supreme effort, he reminded himself why he was here and stepped toward the fireplace. "We must speak," he said. "I knew they wouldn't let me see you. That's why I came in this way," he added with a rueful smile.

Claudia's brow wrinkled. Her head swiveled from side to side. "Did you see a little boy when you came in?"

"No." His gaze cut around the dusky chamber. "Should I have?"

"He was here a moment ago." Claudia climbed back on the window seat and looked at the sinking moon before turning her eyes earthward. Then she took several faltering steps to the bed and began flinging pillows this way and that.

Briefly, he had a flash of his own sleepwalking misadventures. Is that what was happening here? When he reached her, she'd discarded all the pillows and was starting on the covers.

He reached around her and grasped her wrists. His body curled protectively over her back. She fit just right against him. The cleft between the sweet curves of her buttocks cradled him softly. He bit back a groan.

"Claudia, stop," he spoke into her ear. Her clean, fresh smell wafted from her skin to drug his senses like a potent liqueur. "Who are you looking for? There's no boy here."

"Oh, he was!" She turned in his arms, pivoting on a knee. Her hands skimmed up his front and hooked around his neck. "His name is Elbow, and he's made of marmalade. He sat beside me and talked for hours and hours." Her words came faster, almost frenzied. As she spoke, she nuzzled her face into his neck. "I wanted to give him a sweet for keeping me such good company."

She butted her head beneath his chin and rubbed, like a cat demanding to be petted. And God help him, he petted her. He lifted her night rail and slid his palms along the outside of her silky thighs. There wasn't a blessed stitch beneath her gown, nothing to keep him from touching his fill of her warm, satin skin.

"Kiss me, Henry, please," she murmured.

He hesitated, even as his blood pounded in his ears and called him three kinds of fool for wasting time. "Claudia," he said, his fingers kneading their way up her spine, "did you take some medicine tonight?"

"Mr. Whombleby gave me laudanum. I didn't want to drink it, but it seemed important to Mama that I rest. And I couldn't let them know about the blood."

An icy fist slammed into his sternum. All the air rushed from his lungs and his vision narrowed to pinpricks. Henry yanked his hands away. How could he touch her? How could he allow himself to dream of anything intimate with Claudia, after what he'd done? She'd been so injured, the surgeon had to give her drugs to ease her pain and help her sleep. Once again, he saw the bloody sheets. He imagined torn, tender flesh, tissues ripped asunder by his own depraved lust.

Claudia, still half-drugged, let out a piteous whimper when he stepped away. "Don't! Oh, don't, Henry. Please come back. I'm sorry. I'm so …" Her voice caught around a strangled sob. "I'm so sorry, Henry." Her voice gasped out on a quick exhalation between wrenching cries. "The blood. I'm so sorry."

He couldn't stand it. He couldn't stand himself. "Don't apologize!" He grabbed her shoulders and shook her once. "Don't you dare try to take this away from me. It's my fault, Claudia. Mine alone. I'm the one who's sorry. I don't deserve your forgiveness, but I'm going to try to get it. Whatever it takes. I just—" He swallowed around an unfamiliar burn in his throat. "I need to know you don't hate me."

She sniffled. "How could I hate you?" She lifted the hem of her night rail and used it to pat her eyes and wipe her nose. Poor, sleepy lamb, he thought.

"Back to bed with you." He guided her down and tucked the covers around her.

It didn't make sense to try to carry on a conversation with her in this state, but he couldn't resist asking: "Claudia, would you really rather marry Sir Saint than me?"

She shook her head violently, the sound swallowed by the down pillow. "No! I don't want to marry him. I despise the thought of it. I would be terribly unhappy. I'm so scared they'll make me, Henry."

Relief swamped him, releasing a knot between his shoulder blades. Had she preferred the odious Sir Saint to himself, he might have to rethink whether life was worth living.

"Shhhh," he soothed, running the back of his finger along the curve of her jaw. "If you don't want to marry him, then you won't, sweeting, I swear. If I can do nothing else to make things up to you, I'll stop you from having to marry him."

Claudia's watery eyes blinked drowsily, the lids growing heavy as she squirmed deeper into the mattress.

He pressed a kiss to her forehead. "Sleep now, Claudia." His nose skimmed the bridge of hers; then he placed another kiss on the tip. "Sleep, sweetheart." Another brush of his nose, this time just a sweep down the valley of her lip to her Cupid's bow. One small kiss on her lips. Just this one. "Rest, sweet girl." Maybe just one more.

Then the heat between them quickened. Her fingers raced to his neck, cupped the back of his head, held him against her mouth. Her whimper of encouragement rattled in his throat and drove from his mind every thought that wasn't related to this. To her. To his woman.

Claudia tugged his hair. Then again, harder. He welcomed the flash of pain. It felt like atonement.

He kissed her cheek, traversed her cheekbone with the tip of his tongue. His lips and teeth lightly worked around the whorl of her ear. Claudia shuddered beneath him. The bed enticed him with its promise of comfort. Claudia tempted him with her soft welcome. He let his torso fall, pressing her deeper into the bed, so he sheltered her body with his own.

But then, behind his eyes, flashes. Tearing flesh. Pain. A spilling of blood.

Slowly, so as not to startle her, Henry pulled away. His body howled in protest. Never had he been so aroused by a few kisses. Self-loathing mixed with desire in a dreadful alchemy. Here he was, taking advantage of Claudia yet again, this time in full possession of his faculties. What was wrong with him?

And Claudia, poor girl, smiled up at him as though he'd hung the moon. "I knew you'd take care of me. I knew if only I could get to you, everything would be all right." Heavy lids slid home and did not rise again.

Though the laudanum had addled her mind, the sweet sentiment still shone through. His throat tightened at the undeserved show of trust. "I swear, Claudia, I will *always* take care of you."

Chapter Six

Daylight found Henry once again traveling to Rudley Court, this time on horseback by way of the roads rather than dragging landscaping equipment through the woods on foot. His head throbbed in time with his mount's trotting footfalls, as badly as if he'd just crawled out of a barrel of whiskey. It wasn't a hangover that afflicted him, but a lack of sleep and the guilt that had eaten away at him since awaking to a nightmare yesterday morning.

The good thing about sleep deprivation, Henry decided as he passed the reins to a groom, was that it lent him a certain measure of detachment. He witnessed everything around him through a fuzzy haze. He also didn't have to work to achieve his grim expression. He very well might fall flat on his face from exhaustion, which was no laughing matter.

When Ferguson answered the door, he glowered at Henry before letting out a sigh of long-suffering. "I've been instructed not to admit you, Mr. De Vere. I'm sorry."

"Never would I ask you to countermand instructions, Ferguson. Perhaps we could try this again? When I knock this time, send someone else along, and then it won't be you admitting me."

"I could not do that, sir," the butler said. He shifted on his feet and looked uncomfortable in his attire, a first for the implacable servant. Henry suspected he was very close to winning the butler over to his side. After all, Ferguson had always been something of a gruff uncle to the Baxter children—and himself, by extension.

Changing tack, Henry arranged his face in a pleading expression. "Ferguson, by now, you know what happened." The servants always knew. "I'm trying to do right by Miss Claudia, and so I must speak with Sir John. Surely, you want to see all of this sorted out?"

The old retainer's tongue poked a lump in one cheek, which moved about ponderously while the older man stared up the drive. "Mr. De Vere," he finally said, straightening, "I will not allow you to enter Rudley Court, nor can I spare another moment for you. The silver must be polished. In the back pantry. I very sincerely hope not to be disturbed by you again this morning."

With a sharp nod, Ferguson slammed the door in Henry's face. The lock did not turn.

Henry smiled. *Clever old devil.*

After allowing enough time for the butler to vacate the area, Henry let himself in. He found Sir John in the study, seated at his desk. Also present was Sir Saint Tuggle. Today, the old fop wore a pink wig to compliment his mauve costume. Falls of lace, yellowed with age, spilled from his wrists and throat. The fabric at his neck blended with his jowls, which were the color of congealed porridge. Mint green stockings and red, heeled shoes completed the ensemble. It was finery meant to awe and intimidate—twenty years ago, at any rate.

Color bloomed across Sir John's cheeks at Henry's abrupt entrance. "What are you doing here? You're not welcome, De Vere, not any more. Remove yourself at once!"

Henry extended his arm in a placating gesture. "Please, Sir John, you don't want to alarm Lady Baxter or Claudia with your shouting. You've every right to your anger, sir, but I would ask you to put your temper aside, so we might rationally discuss the situation."

"We've nothing to speak about," Sir John snapped. He stood and yanked his spectacles from his face. Waggling them at the papers on the desk, he continued, "On the other hand, I have quite a lot to discuss with Sir Saint. Thanks to you, Claudia's marriage contract has to be redrawn."

Henry was tempted to snatch the hated papers and tear them to bits. "That's just it, Sir John. You cannot allow this wedding to take place."

Sir John cocked his head, his eyes narrow and sharp. "I beg your pardon?"

Turning to the other man, Henry gave a polite bow. "Sir Saint, would you please excuse us?"

The old roué's lips pursed. Moisture glistened between them. "What? I should say not! Impudent hellion. Suppose you're still trying to steal my bride, what? Baxter," Tuggle said, leaning forward, his cane gripped in his left hand, "I'm doing you a demmed service by taking your daughter away from this rakehell. Mark my words, you've only seen the start of your trouble with this one, what? Lock the maids up tight at night, before he gets a taste for them."

A flush of anger and embarrassment rose up Henry's neck. He hoped his cravat kept it out of sight of the other men. "So you will not grant me a private interview?" he directed to Sir John.

"No."

"Very well, then." He lifted his chin and rested one arm behind his back. "I had hoped to spare all of us some discomfort by saying this in confidence, but since that is a dream not to be realized …"

Sir John flinched. Henry noticed how wan the older man looked behind a thin veneer of bluster.

Henry couldn't imagine the anguish afflicting Sir John and Lady Baxter right now. For more than thirty years, their lives had revolved around their children. And now, when they finally had the last of them set up for their own adulthoods, disaster. Henry didn't like having to add to Sir John's burdens, but he'd made Claudia a promise.

"Sir John," he said, speaking to Claudia's father as though Tuggle weren't even in the room, "it must have occurred to you that Claudia may, even now, be carrying my child."

Sir John's mouth tightened.

"I would ask you to wait, sir. Please, postpone the wedding until Claudia's state may be definitively determined."

Tuggle's cane thumped against the floor. "I mean to have that girl. All the better if you've done the hard part for me. I'm eager to have this heir business over and done with."

Violence.

The compulsion blinded Henry. He saw nothing but a myriad of ways to bring slow, agonizing pain to Saint Tuggle. He'd start with clamps, he thought, or perhaps an iron maiden. There was something so wonderfully Gothic about the contraption. He could almost see himself stuffing the old sausage of a man into the metal casing. Every prick of agony would be richly deserved.

"I rather think not," he said, his mild tone concealing bloody fantasies.

Sir John frowned. He wiped the lenses of his spectacles with a handkerchief and resettled them on the bridge of his nose. Then he sat behind his desk and sipped from the teacup resting near his elbow.

At last, he spoke. "He's right, Saint. You cannot marry Claudia while she possibly carries a De Vere." The hollow resignation in his voice only slightly dampened Henry's sense of triumph.

Sir Saint sputtered a protest, but Sir John shook his head. "There's no use for it, Tuggle. You know it must be this way. Hopefully, we'll know the truth of things, one way or another, inside a month."

"A month," Sir Saint fumed. "And what if she is carrying De Vere's bastard? Are you going to marry her off to him, the man who ravished her? And what am I supposed to do in the meantime? Sit on my thumb, what?"

Sir John sank into his shoulders. "I'm sorry, Saint. I know this is a disappointment to you. It's a disappointment to us all."

Henry couldn't help the victorious gleam shining in his eyes. "I'm sure you won't have any difficulty procuring a new bride for yourself, Sir Saint. I'd encourage you to run along and find one."

After the gentleman fumed out, his great belly leading the way, Henry once again regarded Sir John. "With your permission, sir, I'd like to court Claudia."

"That would be highly irregular. As far as I'm concerned, she's still engaged to Tuggle."

A muscle in Henry's jaw twitched. "Sir John, I would ask you to reconcile yourself to the fact that I, not Sir Saint, will marry Claudia. She's reached her majority and may marry whom she chooses. She never chose Sir Saint—you did. Claudia went along with the match only because she felt she must."

Sir John lowered his face into his hands. "Henry, don't you think I know you're young and handsome? Do you suppose I just happened to overlook eligible young men next door? Please give me a little more credit than that, son."

"Then why—?"

"Because you've no prospects," said Sir John, raising eyes as weary-looking as Henry felt. "Duncan hasn't much, given the state of that land your father mismanaged, but at least there's a title. Unfortunately, your sire rebuffed my overtures when I approached him about marrying Duncan to one of my girls. Said his heir could do better than a baronet's daughter, so I never raised the subject again, even after Duncan inherited. What have you to offer, Henry? You're a younger son of a minor barony. You've no fortune. How would you even begin to support a wife and family with that minor shipping concern of yours? You're affable enough to liven up a party, but you aren't precisely marriageable.

"Tuggle may be as old as I, but he's richer than Lady Baxter's Christmas gravy. Sooner or later, he'll make Claudia a wealthy widow, and she'll be free to do as she likes. All told, it's a much neater plan than any other offer she's received, which is precisely none."

Behind his back, Henry's fingers clenched and released. "Thank you for your candor," he said. "I hope you know I've always respected you and your good opinion, Sir John."

The older man snorted.

"Allow me to assure you," Henry continued, "I will be able to comfortably support Claudia and our future children. As you so accurately stated," he said with a touch of ice, "the barony Duncan inherited was nothing of which to boast. But over the last two years, Duncan has invested his share of the profits from De Vere and Sons into Fairbrook and improved the estate, while I've put mine right back into the company. We now own two ships. While I've little by way of ready cash, the seeds have been sown for a prosperous future, both for my brother and myself. In the meantime, Duncan would welcome us at Fairbrook. Last night, he assured me Claudia and I are free to use the dower house as long as need be, although I look forward to setting up our own establishment as soon as possible."

Sir John sighed. His shoulders drooped. He seemed bleak, resigned. "I didn't know your little company was doing as well as that. I apologize for casting aspersions. Still, I cannot like this. Not after …" With a shaking hand, he lifted his teacup and took a long sip. "Claude told me about the sleepwalking. Is that truly what happened? I remember the fits you gave your parents when you were a boy, and how you used to bump around here at all hours, but *that*? Is it even possible?"

Henry dropped into the chair Tuggle had vacated. Idly, he toyed with the empty hole in his shirt cuff. "It must be, Sir John. True, I've never heard of such a thing, but I got into all sorts of trouble in my sleep when I was younger. Ate myself sick more than once. Woke up in a tree—that was particularly terrifying. I swear to you, sir, I would never willfully harm Claudia. I've no memory of the incident. You've known me all my life. At this point, you know me better than my own father did. Do you believe me capable of brutalizing your daughter?"

John Baxter's face crumpled. Suddenly, he seemed older and frailer than he'd been a moment ago. "No. No, Henry, I don't." He sighed. "I suppose I must let you court Claudia, mustn't I?"

Given the circumstances, it was difficult to feel any elation at Sir John's acquiescence. Still, as Henry departed the study and went in search of his missing cufflink, he found himself growing more excited.

Even as a boy, he'd mooned over Claudia's big eyes and long hair. She'd been a mischievous wench, but she'd only caused trouble in the name of fun. Her games were the cleverest, her barbs the funniest. Being in Claudia's orbit had always made Henry happy.

Somewhere along the line, he'd gotten used to the idea of Claudia always being there. She'd seemed like such a sure thing, as if she was his by some unspoken rule. Her London Season had been a rude awakening. Even though he couldn't really have her for himself, prior to her come-out, some five years ago, it had never occurred to him that another man might claim her heart. He'd made it to Town for her debut ball where, it seemed, every buck and popinjay in London had danced with her. Afterwards, he'd had to return to university, and had spent several months feeling as though his head was on the chopping block, waiting to hear that some other man had discovered Henry's treasure and scooped her up for himself.

When the Season ended with Claudia still unattached, Henry breathed easier. His condition rendered him unsuitable for matrimony, so he'd contented himself with admiring her from afar. He'd never spoken to her on the subject of his infatuation, never allowed himself to be more than her friend.

As he stepped into the guest room, Henry recalled Claude's accusation that he had bedded Claudia so that he might have her for himself. He'd answered in the negative. But what if, on some deep, underlying level, his dismay over learning about Claudia's imminent marriage to another man *had* triggered the terrible episode? After all, when Claudia told him about her upcoming nuptials, had he not internally reeled at the news? Had he not wanted her to throw over her affianced husband for his sake?

Those reactions, and the horrible thing he'd done while asleep, strongly implied Henry was an absolute scoundrel, the lowest of the low. He could scarcely countenance himself. In no way was he worthy of Claudia, and the only things that stayed him from running away to live on a mountaintop in Tibet were the possibility that she might be pregnant with his child and the fact that he'd promised to keep her out of Tuggle's clutches.

The guest room had been cleaned. The bed was made and if Henry pulled back the counterpane, he would find clean, unbesmirched sheets. Still, just the sight of the large piece of furniture made acid rise in his throat. He'd always slept here when he stayed at Rudley Court, but he would have to request a different chamber for future visits. This one was ruined for him.

A glance around the floor didn't turn up his missing cufflink. If a maid found it, it might have been handed over to Ferguson for safekeeping. With all the scuffing about in the room the other day, perhaps it had been kicked under a piece of furniture. Dropping to hands and knees, he crawled to look under the washstand. Nothing. The wardrobe, perhaps? No.

Then he remembered he'd placed the cufflinks on the bedside stand when he undressed. He circled around the bed and looked beneath that small table. Not there, either. With a frustrated growl, he turned his head to look under the bed. A telltale golden glint caught his eye. "Ho! Success!" he crowed. The cufflink was beside another object.

Henry fished them both out. He affixed the cufflink to his shirt, then, curious, turned his attention to the other item. It was a small bottle, made of green glass. Cautiously, he sniffed at the opening and drew back at the metallic tang. He brought the bottle to the window for a closer examination. The container was empty, save for a residual ring around the bottom. Though it had discolored in drying, the substance was unmistakably blood.

He let out a rush of air, as though he'd been punched in the gut. His lips went cold an instant before the feeling of betrayal whipped through him like a wild storm. The bottle vibrated to a blur in his shaking hand, but he didn't need to inspect it any more closely; Henry knew what had happened.

Claudia Baxter had trapped him.

• • •

At a table in the library, Claude bent over a mountain of ledgers and correspondence. He was preparing to take on the post of steward at Sheerness Downs, an estate in the neighboring county, and, despite the intensity of her glare, seemed quite oblivious to her boring into the top of his head. So much for that special twin connection.

Claudia watched her brother work with pangs of envy and regret. She couldn't help feeling jealous that he was about to embark on a new life. As far down the line of Baxters as he was, Claude had no choice but to earn his own living. After studying husbandry and finance in school, he'd come home to learn from Sir John everything there was to know about running an estate. Now, he was absorbing as much knowledge about his future home as he could cram into his head. He waited only for Claudia's wedding; then he'd be off, leaving her behind.

She glanced at the book in her lap, Byron's latest, and saw she hadn't turned the page in half an hour.

It was a strange kind of grief to think of her twin being so far away. Though they'd been separated before, it was always with the understanding that the parting was temporary. Deep down,

Claudia always knew her brother would be back. This time, though, the visits home would be temporary reunions. Separation would be their normal state of being.

Absently, she pulled a hank of her hair—loose but for the ribbon holding it back from her face—and began twisting it. "Claude?"

"Yes, Claude?" he replied without looking up.

Claudia smiled. Lady Baxter despised how the twins referred to one another by the same name, but Claudia, at the wise old age of six, had very matter-of-factly informed her mother she should have thought of that before giving them nearly identical appellations. It only worked amongst the two of them. Too much confusion arose when other family members had tried to adopt the pet moniker for Claudia, and so it was her brother's alone.

"Nothing, I just wanted to hear you say it." She set aside her book and strolled to where he worked. "Soon you'll be gone, and no one will call me that ever again." She wrapped her arms around his shoulders and hugged.

Claude patted her arm. "I'll only be in Somerset, not Outer Mongolia." He turned in his seat and scrutinized her face. "You're awfully maudlin. Are you feeling well? Perhaps you should go back to bed."

She let her tongue hang from her mouth as she made a gagging sound. "No more bed! I spent most of yesterday in it, and slept every bit of twelve hours last night, thanks to Mr. Whombleby's dreadful laudanum."

And what a strange night it had been, riddled with wild dreams that left her lethargic. They'd all felt so real, hallucinations, she supposed, caused by the opium. A parade of visitors had tromped through her room, from a child made of marmalade to Henry.

There was no explaining the marmalade dream, but her Henry hallucination must have been brought on by thinking of him so much. She still couldn't stop puzzling over his behavior on the balcony yesterday, his apologies and sadness.

"May I ask you something?" she said before she could think better of her course.

"Certainly." Claude had resumed his inspection of tenant farm reports, but glanced up at her. "What is it?"

"Men enjoy the company of women, don't they? Intimately, I mean."

Her brother winced. "No, we are not talking about this. Go ask Mother."

"It's just," she pressed, her fingers knotted at her waist, "I wonder …" She tripped over her words, fumbling for a way around to her real question. "… *if* they do, why some men, like Sir Saint, wait so long for marriage."

A laugh burst from his throat. "Are you asking if Sir Saint Tuggle is a virgin? Whether he will come to your marriage bed pure and unsullied?"

She nodded.

Claude smirked. "It's different for men, Claude. We aren't held to the same standards as ladies. Unless he's the saint his mother hoped him to be—and I assure you, that is not the case—then I don't see how he could possibly be … you know."

When she didn't say anything, he returned to his work.

Claudia crossed an arm over her middle, rested her other elbow on it, and tapped her chin. "So, are you telling me that you—"

"*Argh!* Stop it! No more!"

"But what about Henry?" she demanded. She had to get the answer out of her brother before he ran her off. "Do you think he's untouched? Before the other night?"

He clapped his hands over his ears. "For the love of God, Claudia! You couldn't find an able-bodied man over the age of eighteen who is not experienced. Does that satisfy you? Christ, woman! Go away and let me work in peace."

"Mercy, you needn't get so ruffled. We've always been able to talk about anything."

"Not this!"

Claudia huffed.

There was a knock. The twins both looked as the door opened. Henry paused in the entry. "Greetings, Baxters."

Butterflies buffeted Claudia's stomach. Ever since The Plan, she couldn't put Henry back in the proper compartment of her mind. Years ago, she'd trained herself to regard him as no more than a friend, but the last thirty-six hours had thrown her mind into total disarray. Once again, Henry was the hero of her romantic fantasies. She'd woken to his kisses yesterday, and dreamed of kissing him again last night.

He was so handsome it made her teeth ache. Today, he wore a dark blue coat, which made his hair look like antique gold. His linen was crisp and white at his throat. Nankeen breeches clung to thighs heavily muscled by years of avid horsemanship. Even his calves looked powerful, encased in brown riding boots. Goodness, but he was delectable.

"You're dressed to ride," Claude observed. "Thank God. You've arrived not a moment too soon." He cut a meaningful look at his sister. "Give me a moment to put these things away and we'll be off."

"Actually, Claude, I hoped I might persuade Miss Baxter to accompany me."

Yesterday's grim demeanor remained in the past, Claudia was pleased to note. Henry held himself straight and tall, one hand behind his back, the other resting on his thigh. The perfect sporting gentleman.

When his gaze came to rest on her, however, Claudia recoiled. There was something wrong with his eyes. An unfathomable emotion. Or rather, a lack of one. Henry could never hide anything from her. She'd grown up reading his face. Every tic of his brow betrayed interest or annoyance. Every quirk of a lip told her what amused him. She could read his nose twitches like a fortune teller read tea leaves—whether he was trying to suppress a sneeze, had smelled something unpleasant, was bored with a conversation, or knew she was beating him at chess. She could write chapters about his face, the various ways he communicated without uttering a sound.

"I'm not sure that would be prudent," Claude protested. "After what happened—"

"Come now, Claude," Henry bit, "I'm wide awake. What could happen?"

Claudia frowned. What did being awake have to do with anything?

"How about it, Claudia?" Henry's voice imitated pleasantness but lacked any real emotion, just like his face. "Will you come, or will you continue gawking at me all day?"

She stared. And he stared back.

She didn't meet his eyes. Dismissing the orbs themselves as useless at present, Claudia's gaze roamed his face. Brows to lips to nose to cheek to chin. This blankness was alien, unnatural. It couldn't continue forever. He couldn't lock her out … There. Finally. At his temple, a muscle twitched.

He was upset with her. She could deal with upset, now that she knew. At least he seemed willing to give her the chance to explain herself.

She beamed, hoping to lift his spirits and start mending their friendship. "I'd be delighted to accompany you, Henry."

But when he smiled back, it was an expression so false she couldn't bear to look at him another moment.

Her own smile slipped. This was going to be a fun ride. Oh, well. It would be worth a little unpleasantness to make things right.

Chapter Seven

When Claudia met Henry outside the stable some forty-five minutes later, he was adjusting his horse's bridle and conversing with a groom. Claudia paused for a moment to admire his profile. Straight nose, strong jaw, and high cheekbones presented a pleasing array of masculine angles. His brows looked as though they'd been dashed across his face by an artist with a devil-may-care attitude. Even his top lip came to a firm V in the middle, but the bottom lip was softer, and when he turned on her with a smile, that sensual curve seemed to tell her all sorts of wicked secrets.

As she approached, Henry's jaw slackened for just an instant before he snapped it shut. A flurry of nerves rocked through her, but Claudia lifted her chin. She knew she looked her best—which wasn't saying much, if one were to compare her to London's fashionable ladies. But with no one but the grooms and Pepper, the three-legged stable cat, vying for immediate competition, she wasn't a total antidote, either.

After accepting Henry's invitation, she'd torn up the stairs to her bedchamber and summoned the maid who attended both Claudia and Lady Baxter. The servant deftly worked the sides of Claudia's hair into braids which met at the crown of her head. The rest was twisted, tucked, and pinned into a chignon, with a few strands loosened and curled to frame her face. Claudia donned a white shirt and cravat, topped with her new riding habit of buttery yellow and kid gloves. The brim of her black hat dipped low in the front, while the jonquil ribbon tied around the crown fell in twin streamers halfway down her back.

When she reached him, Henry kissed her hand while maintaining eye contact, his gaze still cold. "My very dear Miss Baxter," he murmured. Then he flipped her hand and nipped a patch of exposed skin on the inside of her wrist. His tongue soothed the tiny sting.

Claudia jerked her hand back, discomfited by the way he stirred her blood, even as his distant demeanor warned her away. She turned to greet her horse, Coco, who nickered when she caught sight of Claudia. The little mare was a dark bay, with a white blaze and glossy black mane and tail. Claudia dug a lump of sugar from her pocket and offered it on her palm. Coco daintily took the treat. "Hullo, dear girl," Claudia said. "What do you think? Shall we grace these smelly males with the pleasure of our company?"

Beside Coco, Henry's new piebald gelding, Lava, turned his head away and blew out, as though offended. Claudia laughed. Behind her, Henry's hands settled on her waist. "Ready?" he asked. He pressed against her back before boosting her to the saddle. To the casual observer, it was just a few seconds of contact, but Claudia felt the mark of his touch on her body well after he'd settled onto his mount and led her out of the stable yard.

They rode in silence for a time, along a ridge overlooking a field awash in the vibrant yellow of rape flowers. In the distance, stone cottages dotted the landscape. The fresh air and sunshine did much to clear away the mental cobwebs left behind by Mr. Whombleby's opium tonic. Claudia did not think she could tolerate another pointless dose, not even to appease her mother. Thankfully, Claudia had managed to convince her parent she felt well this morning.

Henry drew his horse to a stop and Claudia pulled up alongside. Coco shifted, causing Claudia's skirt to brush against Henry's leg. He laid a hand on her knee and asked, "How are you, Claudia? Quite recovered? Sitting a horse does not cause undue discomfort, I trust?"

His inquiry sounded like mockery. Claudia blanched. How unlike himself Henry was behaving! "My chief complaint is the laudanum I was pressed to take."

"Dreadful stuff." He gave an exaggerated shudder. "Best reserved for grievous pains. You must have been in a bad way."

"Nothing extraordinary. It was all very usual, I assure you."

He nodded gravely. "Yes, I see. The usual dose of medication to stop the hurts of typical intercourse. It's a wonder ladies' little musical and literary societies are not fronts for opium dens, given the many hurts they must suffer." A bitter sneer contorted his features.

"Only the first time," Claudia rushed. Why did he persist in the charade of having lain with her, even here, in private? It was a great mystery, but the cold aloofness of his demeanor forbade that line of questioning. "The dreams were the most disturbing I ever experienced. Each one so vivid, I could have sworn it was real. I dreamt the posts of my bed were all arguing with one another over which did the most work in supporting the canopy. What a strange vision! How does one's mind even concoct such a thing? And then—" She halted, brought up short by the recollection of one of her last dreams of the night. Henry had been in her room. He'd flown in and kissed and held her until her body sang for his attentions.

His eyes blazed. "And then what?" Awareness pulsed between them, as though he knew her mind.

But she could not reveal such mortifying fancies. "What say you to a race?"

He scoffed, seeming to soften a bit. "Coward."

She pointed to a path, which led through a wooded area, down a gentle slope toward the Avon. "To the riverbank," she said.

"What is the forfeit?" he asked.

"If I win—"

"Not going to happen." She hoped his confident teasing marked a turn in his mood. "*When* I win, I shall claim my prize at the finish. Ready?"

They leaned over their horses' necks. Claudia gave the word, and they were off.

Coco plunged forward. Claudia whispered encouragement in the mare's ear. Beside her, Henry started to pull ahead, his mount churning up black clods of earth. The spirited mare would have none of that, straining at the bit to keep pace with Lava.

The trees flew past in a blur and each of Coco's strides ate up ground. A low branch jutting out around a curve caught Claudia off guard. She yelped and threw herself flat against her horse to avoid hitting it. The mishap gave Henry the opening he needed to take the lead.

Around another bend, the river came into view. Sunlight dappled the surface, throwing brilliant diamonds across her vision. Claudia gloried in the sight, her anxieties momentarily abated as she reveled in the thrill of the race.

There was nothing for it, though. The tree branch had cost her the win, and Henry was already dismounting when Claudia and Coco met them at the river's edge. The piebald whinnied a greeting to the mare. Coco cut the grass with a hoof and vocalized in reply.

Laughing and breathless, Claudia accepted Henry's help in dismounting. Her hands curled around his strong shoulders as he lifted her out of the saddle. The wild gleam in his eyes made Claudia's toes curl inside her half-boots. His face had a healthy color, and his hair was delectably wind tousled. He seemed so much more in his usual, easy humor. It was worth losing the race just to restore his mood.

"I trounced you, just as I knew I would." The words were teasing, as she would have expected, but his tone was brittle.

His hands held firm on her waist. Claudia's heart, already pounding from the exhilaration of exercise, thumped madly against her ribs. "Congratulations, Henry," she said. "What do you choose for your prize?" She glanced at him from beneath her lashes.

His lips, smooth and cool, brushed over hers. "Don't play the coquette, Claudia." He released her and walked to the horses. Unbridled and loosely tethered to a nearby tree, the beasts could drink from the cool, flowing river and chomp the new, sweet grass. With the animals tended, Henry peeled off his gloves and frock coat, hooked a finger in the collar, and tossed it over his shoulder. He sauntered toward the shade of a willow tree; its draping canopy trailed verdant fingertips into the river.

Claudia followed, beckoned by the cool grass. Henry spread his coat on the ground and gestured gallantly. Grinning, she took his hand and folded her legs beneath her.

"Ah-ah," he chided. "No shoes on my coat, please."

"There, I've rearranged myself." She divested herself of hat and gloves, which she set at the base of the trunk. "Soft grass just begs for bare toes, doesn't it?"

Henry reached for her foot and made short work of the bootlaces. With a mighty heave, he wrenched the half-boot from her foot. "Henry DeVere," she said with laughing warmth, "not only have you breached propriety by removing an article of my clothing, I feel quite earnestly there was an insult in the way you went about it. Is my foot too large for my boot? Do you accuse me of forcing myself into a smaller shoe for the sake of vanity?"

Just like that, his relaxed smile was gone. "Forcing yourself? Oh no, Claudia, I doubt you, of all people, would ever countenance any kind of force." His eyes and mouth tightened as he quickly removed her other shoe. "Take off your stockings, Claudia."

Her mouth went dry. "Wh-what?"

"So you can enjoy the grass between your toes," he clarified. "Take off your stockings."

Awkwardly, she turned her back to him and did so. Her face flamed as though fevered. There was something decisive about this moment, she recognized. Her stomach trembled with nerves—or was it anticipation?

When she turned back to him, he glanced at her feet and the flash of exposed ankles. "Now for my forfeit."

"Was that kiss not the prize?"

One side of his mouth drew up in a lazy smile. "That was not a kiss. I trust I made a better account of myself than that two nights ago."

How was she to respond?

After a beat, Henry dragged the top of a fingernail down one of her feet. Claudia's toes curled. "Your bare feet are going to waste on my coat. You've come this far, Claudia. Take your pleasure."

His voice was an invitation to sin. She watched, mesmerized, as he took her ankles, parted them, and guided her feet into the grass on either side of his own knees. Henry's thumbs traced circles on her ankles while his palms cupped the base of her calves. The cool blades tickled her arches, in contrast with his warm touch. "How does that feel?" he asked. "Good?"

She made some inarticulate sound of agreement.

"Your fingers should have the same experience." Henry leaned forward between her thighs and planted his hands atop hers, beside her hips. Thick, square-tipped fingers captured her own. His face occupied the space beside her neck, his breath a warm breeze in her ear. Her heart hammered in her ears. Smoothly, Henry parted his arms, sending Claudia's palms in a slow, sensual slide over the silk lining of his coat and out into the grass.

As her arms spread wider, Claudia tilted back and Henry followed, maintaining a small space between their bodies. He stopped their movement, leaving her back hovering above the ground. Claudia's stomach trembled, both from the exertion of sustaining her position, and from the pleasurable ache elicited by Henry's sensual play.

Not once did Henry's eyes leave hers. Heat built in his green gaze in time with Claudia's own mounting desire. Though they'd moved only inches, Henry's lips parted and he panted lightly. Clearly, he was as affected by this strange almost-embrace as Claudia. Holding this posture compounded the erotic tension between them, until Claudia thought she'd fracture if something did not happen.

"Henry," she whispered. "Please." She stretched her neck, bringing her trembling lips to his jaw. She felt like a supplicant, humbly beseeching with her kiss.

As though he knew just what she needed, Henry released her hands, moving his own to the back of her head and the small of her back. The sudden release of physical pressure was luxurious; she gladly relaxed into his hands. His lips, dry and warm, touched her chin, her cheek, and then paused, lingeringly, on her lips. Little jolts of pleasure darted through her, but her sense of need only increased.

"You're too bound up," he murmured against her mouth. "All neat and prim." His tongue darted out to touch the corner of her lips. "My Claudia should be free and rumpled."

The proprietary tone of his words thrilled her. *His* Claudia. She hummed low in her throat.

He began plucking out her hair pins, eventually leaving only the braids intact, the rest tumbling free down her back.

"Yes," Henry growled, "this is how I like you." His fingers plunged into her hair and twined around the light brown tresses as he drew her close. Claudia clung to his shoulders, the firm muscles there tense beneath her fingers. Henry's mouth worked over hers, thoroughly exploring every part. She thrilled at his masculine possession, his moan of satisfaction rumbling deep inside her own chest. Abruptly, he pushed her away. "Now then …"

Claudia fell onto her back with a little "Oof!" Her hands flopped to the ground beside her head. The backs pressed into the cool grass, while her hair tickled her palms.

Henry drew her skirts up around her thighs. Kneeling between her legs, he reached down to start unfastening the buttons and hooks on the front of her riding habit.

The feeling of fresh air hitting her heated flesh brought Claudia back to earth. "Wait," she protested. "We mustn't."

Henry's fingers never slowed in their work, methodically peeling her clothes away. "Why not?" he said. "We've already been together, and we'll soon be married. It's all settled." He ran his hands over her ribs. "Stays? Damnation, you really are trussed. Sit up."

Being quickly pulled upright made Claudia dizzy; she couldn't think clearly. "Nothing is settled! I said I wouldn't marry you." It was no use pretending Henry was only a friend any longer, but she wasn't sure how, exactly, he now fit in her life. And he made it impossible to think straight. His hands seemed everywhere at once, handling her like an overgrown rag doll while he undressed her. Nor did it help when she realized she was pawing at him just as eagerly as he was at her.

He glanced up at her from beneath his lashes, a sly smile pulling his lips to one side. The impish expression was like a caress between her legs. "We'll see about that. Sir John gave his permission for me to court you. In any event, you aren't marrying Tuggle. I've taken care of it, just as I promised I would."

"Just as you ..." A faint memory surfaced, a fragment of her drug-induced dreams. She was kissing Henry. He asked her something about Sir Saint, and then—"You were there," she breathed. "Last night. In my room."

"Naturally. Arms up." Pulling her skirts and chemise from under her bottom, Henry divested Claudia of the last of her clothes.

Henry sat back on his heels, admiring his handiwork. For a long time, he studied her, until Claudia became uncomfortable with his scrutiny and reached to cover herself. "Why were you in my room?"

He grabbed her wrist. "Don't hide from me, Claudia. I came to your room because I needed to see you." He guided her hand to the front of his breeches. "This is what you do to me." Her fingers closed around his hard length. Henry groaned and arched into her hand. "You're so bloody gorgeous, Claudia. Just looking at you makes me wild."

The things he said, the things he was doing—it was all overwhelming. How could this be? Could Henry's feelings for her have changed in just the last couple of days?

The raw hunger in his expression went a ways towards calming her nerves. None of her confusion mattered at a moment like this. However it had happened, this was real. Henry wanted her, as she'd always dreamed.

He released her hand and, slowly, she explored him through his clothes. When she pulled toward the top of his shaft, he hissed. When she drew toward the root, he moaned, his erection twitching against her palm. His eyelids fell to half mast. Claudia thrilled at his reactions to her touch.

His fingers drifted over her collarbones and down her shoulders. Pleasure danced over her skin. "That feels so good," she murmured. "Like my mind is in a warm bath." She wanted Henry to experience all these lovely feelings, so she tugged at the buttons on his fall.

"Not yet," he said, gently removing her questing hands. Henry laid her back. Sweet, earthy smells of grass and soil filled the air.

Henry braced himself over her on his forearms. "About last night." He kissed her lips, then nudged her chin with his nose, tilting her head, giving him access to her neck. His lips scorched her skin, but a gentle breeze cooled the little damp marks. "I needed to make sure you were all right, Claudia."

The aching sweetness of his words almost distracted her from the way his thigh was nudging between her legs, insinuating itself against her aching flesh.

"Of course I'm all right," she said. "Why wouldn't I—Oh!" His leg pressed harder against her mound. Claudia canted her hips to rock against him.

Without preamble, Henry's tongue plunged into her mouth. He kissed her fiercely, nipping her lips and sucking her tongue into his own mouth. Below, his hips undulated in a primal, driving rhythm. She planted her feet and arched, craving more contact.

"I must confess something." He licked his way down her neck. "I can't remember our first time. I was sleepwalking." That wicked tongue flicked a nipple, and then he blew on it, causing it to pebble. "Remind me about it, Claudia. Tell me how we made love."

Her breath froze in her throat; her eyes flew wide. "Oh, God," she whispered as the terrible truth dawned on her. He thought it was all real. The blood, the visit from the surgeon.

"Was it good?" he murmured against her breast. "I must've spent an age right here. I've wanted to get my hands on these for years. God, they're perfect." His mouth latched onto one nipple while the pad of his thumb brushed over the other.

"Henry, wait," she said, but her voice was weak and unconvincing.

"I fear I did not spend enough time readying you," he said when he lifted his head from her breast. His hand came between her legs and cupped her. "I'd never been with a virgin before. If I'd done my business properly, there wouldn't have been so much blood."

Strong fingers parted her folds and stroked her core. With the fresh air swirling about, Claudia could tell just how wet she'd grown there. What on earth? She cried out and tried to close her legs while her face flooded with the heat of embarrassment.

"You're still so innocent," he said. "This is a good thing, sweet. Feel how ready you are for me." One finger dipped inside. Henry spread the moisture up and around her tiny nubbin. Pleasure speared deep into her womb. Whatever he was doing was marvelous. "Your body wants me." His voice dropped a register and rumbled seductively against her throat. "Doesn't it, Claudia? Don't you want me?"

"Yes," she cried. A sob tore from her chest as he fondled her. A second finger plunged in alongside the first. She lifted to meet his hand. "More. Please, Henry, more."

He chuckled and positioned himself between her thighs. He rubbed against her. The friction was divine. "You want me now, sweetheart?"

"Yes!" She scrabbled at his shirt, the waist of his breeches, anywhere she could reach.

"Should I bury my cock in you again?"

"Yes—yes!"

"Turn over," he whispered.

Feeling as though she might shatter into a thousand pieces, Claudia flipped onto her stomach. Henry groaned. He palmed her buttocks and lightly bit her hip. "Henry, please!"

He lay a hand on her thigh. "Shh, be still." Something cold and hard touched her lower back. "I have to get something from the saddlebag. Don't move."

Her head was turned away, and so she followed him by sound. What was he retrieving? Was she really about to lose her virginity here, on the riverbank?

Now that she had a moment to consider the matter, Claudia decided that yes, she really was going to do this. She loved Henry. She'd always loved him. She wanted to share this experience with him.

She smiled a private smile and enjoyed the play of the breeze over her skin. It felt like silk.

The small thing was still on her back. What was it? And what was taking Henry so long?

Just then, she heard the soft, heavy thuds of hooves in motion. Eight of them.

Claudia lifted her head just in time to see Henry De Vere leaving on his horse, with Coco tied to his saddle and placidly following.

She shrieked and shot up. The thing on her back tumbled to the ground. As she lunged for her clothes and cursed Henry with every foul epithet she knew, Claudia glanced at the fallen object.

Chapter Eight

The bottle.

That wretched little vessel of deceit.

Claudia snatched it up and sprinted after Henry. It was no good. He'd set the horses to a trot, and they were already too far away for her to catch up. Just before they vanished around a bend, the light caught Henry sitting tall in his saddle. His golden hair and linen shirtsleeves gleamed, putting her in mind of some heroic white knight, a latter-day Galahad, if Galahad were the sort to debauch maidens and abandon them before coming to the point.

She pulled back her arm and hurled the bottle. "Henry DeVere, come back here!" she shouted. "You spineless, shameless, sotted, pig of a man! I'll never forgive you! I'll cut all your boots to ribbons! I'll put nettles in your bed! I'll … I'll tell your mother what you've done!"

If he heard her litany of threats, he gave no indication. Soon, Claudia was alone, with only the burbling Avon for company. Her entire body felt agitated. Tears stemming from a frustration that went beyond his cruel abandonment coursed unchecked down her face.

A brisk reminder from the wind drew notice to the fact that she was entirely unclothed. And standing in the wide open, beneath God's own sky, where any passerby could spot her.

Trembling, Claudia returned to the willow. She sat on Henry's coat, pulled her knees against her chest, put her head down, and indulged in a moment of self-pity. Her private area was swollen, still pulsing for a lover no longer there. The pressure of her legs against her nipples sent needy darts of sensation through her body.

So welcome only a few minutes ago, Claudia now tried to force her body's responses into quietude.

With a loud sniff, she scrubbed the heels of her hands across her cheeks. Then she dressed, taking great care to return each garment to a state of neat arrangement. Without the help of her maid, there was nothing to be done about her hair. She combed fingers through it, then pinned her hat in place.

What to do with Henry's coat? Even in the throes of bitter turmoil, she couldn't bring herself to leave the stylish cutaway on the ground for the foxes to make merry with. Having grown up wearing someone else's castoffs, Claudia was only too aware of the value of quality attire. Henry might have walked away from his coat without a backward glance, but it would bring a world of joy to a deserving young man in the village. The vicar might know a worthy recipient.

So Claudia gathered the coat and the tattered remains of her pride, and began the long walk home.

She stared at the ground while she cut through a field to reach the road that would bring her to Rudley Court. On her way, she relived every moment of Henry's seduction and desertion, feeling again the flush of excitement and the horrible sting of betrayal.

But she'd deserved it, hadn't she? Henry had believed he'd taken her innocence. That he'd sleepwalked through the event. It all made sense now: his remorse, his proposal of marriage. And then he discovered he'd been duped by an impetuous girl who thought only of escaping an unwanted match. For her sins, he'd been banished from Rudley Court, a house where he'd been welcome all his life.

Claudia realized, in a cruel twist of irony, it was *she* who'd ruined Henry, not the other way around. No wonder he'd served her a taste of the same sauce.

"Halloo, Miss Baxter!"

Hailing her from the seat of a gig was Mrs. Monroe, a genteel widow who resided in the village. Beside her sat her niece, Miss Purdue, who was several years older than Claudia.

"Good morning," Claudia greeted her neighbors. "I trust you ladies are well?"

"Tolerably so, I do thank you for asking," said Mrs. Monroe. "Dearest Anne," she said, patting her niece's arm, "had a dreadful toothache these past two days, but it's quite gone now, isn't it, Anne? I feared we might have to send for the blacksmith to attend her, or even travel to Bristol to consult a dentist. Lady De Vere paid us the great compliment of calling yesterday and recommended clove oil, and bless me, it was just the thing! Not a bit of complaint since yesterday afternoon. Is that not so, Anne?"

"Yes, I'm quite recovered, Aunt," said Miss Purdue.

"Lady De Vere is a font of knowledge," Claudia said. The mention of Henry's mother made her even more aware of the coat folded over her arms. Miss Purdue gave it a quizzical look.

"I'm so glad to hear you're on the mend, Miss Purdue," she said, her fingers clutching tighter into the fine material. "If you'll excuse me, ladies, I must be on my way home …"

"You've quite a ways to go to reach the Court!" exclaimed Mrs. Monroe. "As we approached, I said to Anne, 'Bless me, if that isn't Miss Claudia Baxter! I wonder what could have taken her so far from home, and on foot, too.' But then, you've always been a great walker, have you not, whereas poor Anne has never had the constitution for exercise such as you are accustomed to take. 'Moderation in all things will be the key to Miss Purdue's health.' This was the advice given us by Mr. Whombleby, and I declare it's proven true. I regret we've not room in the gig, or I'd offer to take you up. I'm quite mortified!"

Claudia assured her it was no trouble at all, that she liked nothing so much as a walk on a fine day.

"But you are burdened with a parcel, as well! Is that a length of wool? Oh, no, I see now the stitching of a collar. Is it a coat? I declare, isn't that funny? Not twenty minutes past, just as Anne and I were setting out from the Clarksons', we saw Mr. Henry De Vere ride past in his shirtsleeves, if you can credit it! I said to Anne, 'Though I'm sure he's wearing a very fine weskit, it is shocking to see the whole of it flaunted before the neighborhood!' It's only too bad he didn't come upon you, Miss Baxter, as you might have remedied his astonishing disarray. Why it's quite a coincidence that you should have just the thing—"

Mrs. Monroe's voice slid to a halt, though her final words seemed to ring in the air between Claudia and the gig. Miss Purdue's eyes lit; she smiled gleefully. Mrs. Monroe, on the other hand, paled.

Shame, deep and hot, blossomed through every fiber of Claudia's being. She struggled for words to bring about a dignified escape.

Never one to lose the power of speech for long, Mrs. Monroe rallied to put Claudia out of her misery. "Well, I'm sure I've quite chattered your ear off. And you've such a great distance to walk, we must not delay your progress any longer. Indeed, we must not. Anne, let's away. Good morning, Miss Baxter."

Claudia whipped about and strode as fast as her legs would move. She should've gone back home across the countryside, the same way she and Henry had ridden out, rather than take the road. Despite the slower going, she'd likely not have encountered another soul. Now, she could only hope Mrs. Monroe and Miss Purdue would exercise discretion. If they did not …

Oh, the humiliation. The shame! She trudged onward, feeling as though eyes peered at her from everywhere, full of knowing judgment.

This, then, must be what Henry had suffered. This painful, writhing guilt. The dread of looking another human being in the eyes, for fear of having her misdeeds known.

She must apologize. If it meant groveling at his feet, she must beg his forgiveness for having wronged him so. She loved Henry; knowing she'd caused him such pain only compounded her misery.

Would he believe she'd learned her lesson, that she didn't fault him for his improper teaching method? At least Claudia had been aware of what she was doing. Every step of the way, she chose to allow Henry another kiss, another touch. He might have asked her to disrobe, but it was Claudia herself who began it and who willingly took part. She'd gasped at his ministrations and begged for more.

Henry, however, had had no choice when Claudia came to his bed with that bottle of blood. She'd not granted him so much as the courtesy of consciousness when she decided to change the course of his life. For the first time, Claudia realized the magnitude of her deception and its consequences.

Oh, yes, she had much to atone for.

• • •

"Where did you get that?" Claude demanded.

She thrust the coat at her brother. "Please, just put it in your wardrobe," Claudia begged.

They were alone in Claude's room. Mrs. Baxter was out making calls, and Sir John had gone to the village tavern, The Bull's Horn, for the weekly meeting of his gentlemen's club. He claimed they met to discuss local and national affairs, but Claudia suspected that was just an excuse to raise a pint with friends.

Claude took the coat and shook it out. The dark blue wool had become rumpled.

"I say, isn't this Henry's coat?" Her brother's brows snapped together. "Wasn't he wearing it just this morning?"

"Shh!" Claudia flapped her hands. Even with no chance of being overheard by one of their parents, Claudia instinctively sought secrecy. The realization unnerved her.

"This is what's become of me," she wailed. "I'm an unnatural creature, a woman of shadows and lies. Oh, Claude, you must help me!" She burst into tears.

Her twin guided her to a chair. As she sat, Claudia grabbed Henry's coat back and buried her face in it. Warm and permeated with Henry's scent, it was the next best thing to having his arms around her.

As she started to calm, Claude took the coat away again. "You'll ruin it with tears and snot," he chastised. Her twin had worn clothes belonging to older siblings, as well. He stuffed the stained garment into his walnut wardrobe before turning to regard her, his face creased with concern. "Why do you have Henry's coat? Did he violate you again? I knew that story about sleepwalking was tripe! I'll kill him. Did you kick him in the berries, like I showed you?"

"Violate me?" Claudia snuffled.

He glowered. "That's the name for what happened to you, Claudia. You were forced. Violated. Raped."

"You mean …" she started. "The surgeon? He came because I was … was violated?"

"Why else?" Claude gripped her arms. "Did De Vere hurt you again? You must tell me, Claude. If he's abused you, I won't give him the dignity of a duel. He'll stand trial for his crimes."

"Oh, God," she whispered. "You think … Everyone thinks … *Henry* thought …"

The truth was far worse, far uglier than she'd imagined. Her parents and brother concluded she'd been forced against her will. No wonder Mrs. Baxter had quailed at the sight of the bloody bedclothes. No wonder Mr. Whombleby had come to medicate her supposedly injured body and nerves.

"Does Henry really sleepwalk?" she demanded.

Claude snorted. "Gads, yes. Caused me no end of trouble at Harrow. I was practically his night nurse. Had to sleep with our room key hidden behind a loose bit of baseboard. Can't tell you how many times I woke to find him leaning over me, talking nonsense, or repeating a lecture." He chuffed through his nose. "The man claimed that's what happened with you. Said he didn't remember."

"Oh, no," she moaned. "Poor Henry!" He had been made to believe he had done violence against her while he slept. His grave demeanor, his demands that she not absolve him, his pain. It all made sense ... terrible, awful sense.

Claude's mouth twisted and pinched. "And I believed him. I'm so sorry, Claude. I shouldn't have let him come anywhere near you, not ever again. I blame myself."

She grabbed his hands. "No, Claude, that isn't what happened. Henry didn't hurt me today—or the other night, either." At her brother's incredulous expression, Claudia said, "Sit down. I have something to tell you."

Claudia confessed to her brother about the blood and the bottle. About Henry's proposal and his visit during her opium-hazed night. She told him about Henry's intervention regarding Sir Saint, and about his revenge.

At the end of her sorry tale, Claude gaped at her for long, tense moments.

"Say something," she begged.

"Jesus, Claudia!" he blurted. Claude wiped a hand down his face. "You're either the most naïve bumpkin ever to stumble out of a cornfield, or a conniving bitch. Either way, you're frightening as hell." He raised his hand as though lifting a drink, discovered his hand empty, and saluted her, instead.

"I'm not a … what you said. And I'm not naïve, either," she insisted with a lift of her chin. "I knew what to do." She sniffed. "My execution was just a little off."

The corner of his lips kicked up. He snorted.

"It's not funny!" she wailed.

"Yes, it is," Claude retorted. "That's the funniest damn story I've heard in … ever. I can just see old Mrs. Monroe's face now." He threw back his head and laughed, long, deep, and loud.

"What shall I do?" Claudia demanded. "You're my brother. Help me!"

Claude's laughter slowed to gasping whoops while he caught his breath. He sounded like a braying donkey. She said as much, which just set him off again. Doubled over, he grasped his sides. He fell to the floor, his face beet-red and tears streaming down his cheeks.

"Leave off!"

"I can't!" He pulled his knees up. "Christ, I'll wet myself." But he kept on laughing.

Claudia bore his display with all the bruised dignity she could muster. Finally, his spasms of hilarity subsided to chortles and sighs.

"That's your ration of jollies for the coming year. Have you stained yourself?" she inquired, brow lifted.

Claude shook his head. "Pride intact." He jumped to his feet and reached for Claudia's hand. "Sister mine," he said as he hauled her to standing, "you did a terrible thing. It's a hilarious story, but it wouldn't be any wonder if Henry wanted to throttle the daylights out of you. Not that I'd ever permit him to, of course. I'd strike him down before he ever laid a finger on you in violence."

She pinched his nose and waggled his head back and forth. "You're a bloodthirsty brute," she said with a great deal of affection. "Always ready to lay waste to my malefactors. Sadly, I'm the wrongdoer this time."

"You really are," he agreed with good cheer. "You should have seen the woeful state Henry was in when he realized he'd defiled you—or thought he had. Putting a fellow through that kind of hell was badly done of you, Claudia. And I thought you had a care for Henry."

"I have more than a care," she exclaimed. She was brimming with love and sorrow, so full of them she worried her emotions would leak through her skin. She looked into the eyes of her twin, trusting their close bond to communicate what words could not express.

Claude sighed. "If that's the way of it, come on. I'd better take you to see him."

• • •

After returning to her room to set her hair and clothes to rights, Claudia collected her brother. The twins Baxter presented themselves at Fairbrook in time for tea.

They were received by Henry's elder brother, Duncan, who informed them Henry had departed not two hours past to escort their mother to her sister's home in Bristol. The news caused Claudia no small degree of anxiety. How could she apologize to the obstinate man when he'd absented himself?

She considered writing a letter, but this suggestion earned her a censorious frown from Claude.

"Haven't you landed Henry in enough trouble?" Claude asked as they walked home again, with Coco in their company. When they'd collected the mare from Fairbrook's stables, Claudia had felt the questioning glances of the grooms. "Would you further embarrass him in front of his mother and aunt?"

Claudia squirmed. Naturally, she knew correspondence between unmarried young ladies and gentlemen was frowned upon, but considering all the evils heretofore perpetrated, of what import was one more offense? "When did you become an arbiter of etiquette? Besides, don't you suppose, in this one instance, my good intentions outweigh the impropriety?"

A world-weary sigh answered her questions. "Has it not occurred to you," Claude drawled as they reached the top of Rudley Court's long drive, "that Henry might have abruptly left Fairbrook to get away from you, sister?"

In fact, it had not occurred to her. She made a stricken sound. "Well then, what shall I do?"

Claude patted Coco's neck. "Give him time and space, Claudia. That's all you can do. He'll be home soon enough."

Chapter Nine

"Supper was excellent," Henry told his hostess. "Another splendid meal."

Around the table, four more males offered their compliments and groans of satisfaction.

"Having a married friend isn't so bad, after all," said Lord Sheridan Zouche. "One never leaves Mrs. Dewhurst's table regretting having sat down at it, which cannot be said for many a house in Mayfair."

Norman Wynford-Scott chuckled. "Here, here," boomed his deep voice. "I don't mind making the trip from Town for such a gratifying reprieve from the poor fare they foist upon us at the Inns of Court."

"To Mrs. Dewhurst," proclaimed Harrison Dyer, lifting his wine glass in a toast.

"To Mrs. Dewhurst," chorused the rest of The Honorables.

Brandon, seated at the head of the table and husband of their lauded hostess, tipped his glass in a private salute. "To my own Mrs. Dewhurst."

Lorna Dewhurst ducked her head, her freckled cheeks made pink by so much attention. "Thank you, gentlemen, but it's Cook who deserves your approbation."

"Sissy, what's app-ro-bay-shun?" asked the child seated to her left.

"It means 'compliment' or 'approval,' Daniel."

The boy, who, at the tender age of eight, outranked everyone else in the room, tilted his head, his lips screwed up in thought. Then he smiled. "You all get an *approbation* from me for being so nice to Sissy."

The men chuckled and rapped their knuckles on the table.

"All right," Lorna said. "Come along, Daniel. It's time for bed."

The men rose as Lorna stood. Daniel made his way around the table, bidding each gentleman a good night. Harrison and Norman both shook hands with the lad. Sheri gave him a sharp bow and a very correct, "Good evening, my Lord Chorley," which sent Daniel into peals of delighted laughter. Brandon bent to give his young brother-in-law a hug, a sight that had the other Honorables raising their brows at one another. Half a year of marriage had wrought quite a change in their friend, whose profession as a surgeon had heretofore kept him a bit detached from others.

When the boy baron came to Henry, he butted his head into Henry's stomach.

"Daniel!" Lorna gasped. "No!"

Henry gamely clutched his abdomen and let out a dramatic groan. "*Oooo!* I am slain. Gored by the fiercest bull in Toledo." Then he wrapped an arm around the lad's head and ruffled his hair.

Squealing, Daniel squirmed out of his grasp. "We'll play again tomorrow, won't we, Henry?"

"I will be avenged!" Henry proclaimed, finger raised. Then he grinned. "Sleep well, Dan."

As Lorna led Daniel from the dining room, Henry turned to find his friends' attention had settled on him. "What?"

"The fiercest bull in Toledo?" asked Norman, brow raised.

"Henry and Dan, is it?" Sheri drawled. His quizzing glass made an appearance before his eye as Sheri trained his gaze on Henry. "On rather intimate terms with the local aristocracy, I see."

Henry scoffed. "Oh, stuff it, the lot of you. The boy needs companions. Brandon doesn't mind that I play with the lad, do you, Bran?"

"Of course not," said their host, as he led the men from the dining room to the library. There, he poured a measure of Madeira for each of them, the fortified wine having been recently imported by De Vere and Sons.

Looking around the room at his friends made Henry feel a little nostalgic for the old days in Oxford. Back then, The Honorables met at The Hog's Teeth tavern, where they'd quaffed cheap ale and cheaper gin. It was there that they'd given their group a name, *The Honorables* being an acknowledgment of the fact that despite their noble lineages, none of the five friends stood in line to inherit their families' titles. Rather, each bore the legal title The Honorable. Even Sheri was only Lord Sheridan by courtesy. On legal documents, he was The Honorable Mr. Sheridan Zouche, just like the rest of them.

"What I do mind," Brandon said, snapping Henry out of his reverie, "is the fact that you've been at Elmwood for nearly two weeks now, with no explanation as to the purpose of your unexpected visit, nor any indication of when you might away."

Henry shifted in his seat. "Can't a fellow visit friends just because he enjoys their company? If I'm an imposition here, Bran, I'll leave at once." Although, it was a little rich for Brandon to insinuate Henry was not welcome, not when he'd invited the rest of The Honorables out to spend a couple days in the country with them.

"Smooth your hackles, De Vere," Brandon said, one hand extended. "You are always welcome here. Lorna enjoys your society immensely, and Daniel will be inconsolable when you go. If it were up to him, he'd install you in the nursery as his live-in playmate."

Norman cleared his throat and propped his chin on one of his large fists. "Henry, what Brandon is trying to get around to is that—and please tell me if I'm misrepresenting your opinion, Dewhurst—is that you seem to be hiding from something here at Elmwood. Brandon says you've not spoken to him about whatever it is that's got you in a lather, nor have you confided in any of the rest of us via correspondence."

Henry's lips pinched. "So you've all decided to descend upon me *en masse* and make me ... what? Bare my soul?" He leveled an angry glare upon each of his friends—*friends*, hah!—in turn. "And what makes you so sure I have some deep secret weighing heavy on my mind and heart, hmm? If anyone has a secret to share, it'll be you, Norman." He jabbed a finger at his large friend. *Friend ...* hah! "No one should be that tall. Or that calm all the time. It's unnatural."

A heavy sigh was the big man's only response.

"Henry." It was Harrison's quiet voice. He sat on the edge of the glow cast by the fire on the grate, half of his face in shadow. "We've known you a long time. We'd like to help you, if we can."

"Well, it's obviously a woman," Sheri announced. With the hand holding his glass of wine, he made circular gestures in Henry's direction. "Just look at him. Tell me he doesn't have that same, tragic air Brandon had when he wasn't sure about Miss Robbins."

The others scrutinized Henry as though he was one of Brandon's surgical specimens under glass. Damn Sheri and his preternatural sense about women!

"By Jove, I think you're right," Brandon murmured. "Lorna said she thought it would be a woman, but I told her no, Henry would take to falling in love like a duck to water. Hmm." He frowned. "It appears I was wrong."

"Yes," Henry said, throwing his hands wide, "you were wrong. Well done, my fine fellows, you have found me out. I'm laid low by my love for a woman. Congratulations to you all." He lifted his glass in a mocking salute. "Truly. I mean it." He tipped back his drink and drained the contents.

"Is it that country girl of yours?" Sheri asked. "Miss Baxter?"

"Of course it is."

Sheri turned in his seat. "I knew it must be," he told Harrison. "They've been friends since childhood. It's sickeningly perfect."

And it *was* sickeningly perfect. Or it would have been, Henry thought bitterly, if Claudia hadn't misled him in the cruelest way imaginable.

"So now you know," he said. "I'm in love with Miss Baxter, but I haven't yet the security to propose. Being near her, but unable to lay claim to her, was driving me mad. So I came here." Henry dearly hoped the men would accept his explanation and leave off their interrogation.

Sheri nodded. "Just as I thought." He stood and smoothed a hand over his waistcoat. "Gentlemen," he said, giving the room a mocking bow, "I bid you all a good night. And to you, young Henry, I offer my condolences." He clapped a hand on Henry's shoulder. "I'd hoped, being the youngest of us all, you'd have kept me company in bachelordom longer than the rest of these good chaps. Alas, as in nature, it is the young and the weak who are picked off the herd first." He shot a look at Brandon then strolled from the room.

"Well," Norman said after a moment, "on that note, it's bed for me, as well. I must head back to London first thing. I'm helping prepare a case and have to meet with the barrister at noon."

Brandon was next to go, making excuses of tiredness, but obviously just eager to join his wife.

That left Henry and Harrison. The two men sat in silence for a time. "Just like the old days," Henry said.

"Being left behind, you mean?"

Henry nodded. Not only had Harrison and Henry lodged together during university, the other three men were older, and went down from Oxford two years before the others. Henry loved all of The Honorables as brothers, but the bond he shared with Harrison was closer than the rest.

Harrison got up and retrieved the decanter of Madeira from the sideboard. He refilled Henry's glass, and then his own.

"Have you thought any more about coming to work for me?" Henry asked.

"Henry."

"I know it's not the horse farm you want, but I haven't got one of those lying about. I really think, though, that within a few years, you'll have the capital you need to buy yourself a pretty piece of land and the ponies to begin your stock."

"Hen."

"We're pushing east, and I could really use a good man I know and trust to—"

"Henry!"

At last, Henry's eyes snapped to Harrison. His friend's brown gaze was bemused. "What the hell are you going on about?"

Henry rubbed his forehead, sighed. It was no use trying to prevaricate with Harrison. "She set me up."

Harrison paused with his glass halfway to his mouth. "How so?"

Fortifying himself with a long swallow of wine, Henry explained everything. He told Harrison about waking up to a bed full of Claudia and blood, and what he—and everyone else—thought he'd done. What she'd *made* them think he'd done. How he spent the next two days in hell, convinced the Baxter clan would be justified in having him castrated, drawn, and quartered—and that he wouldn't even have tried to stop them. Only his driving need to try to make things right with Claudia, especially if she was with child, had kept him from throwing himself off the nearest cliff.

"It was utterly devastating," he said, "thinking that I'd hurt her—*her*. My Claudia. My girl." He cast a pained look at Harrison. His friend was leaned forward, forearms propped on his knees, his steady, serene gaze a sharp contrast to Henry's agitation.

Hopping to his feet, Henry paced to a bookshelf, pulled out a volume at random, then shoved it back in place. "How could she do that to me? It was everything I used to hate and fear about myself. It was humiliating. It was—"

"It was like Kitty Newman all over again," Harrison interjected.

Involuntarily, Henry's shoulders hunched. "Yes," he quietly agreed. "Like Kitty Newman. But worse."

The other Honorables had long known about Henry's somnambulism, but only Harrison knew the details of Henry's disastrous encounter with the courtesan all those years ago.

"I'm surprised you remember her name," Henry said. "You were good enough never to mention it again, and God knows I've tried my best to forget."

"It was a memorable story." Harrison's tone was dry. "Although you never did say what you did to her slippers."

Henry barked a laugh. "Nor will I." He stood in front of the fire and stared into the glowing depths. His eyeballs seemed to draw back into the sockets at the heat; Henry forced his lids to remain open. "Did you know, I've kept the vow I made that night? That was the only time I ever attempted to sleep with a woman? I mean, actually *sleep*. There's been coitus, of course, but slumber is always a solo event. This thing with Claudia just goes to show why I've been right to avoid it."

"But nothing happened."

Rounding on his friend, Henry issued a scoff of incredulity. "Nothing happened? Did you hear a single word I've just said?"

Rising, Harrison came to stand next to Henry, his palms extended to the fireplace. Snakes of light danced through his dark blond hair, which was on the long side, like Henry's. "I heard you tell a tale of falsehoods. You did nothing wrong, Henry. In fact, I'd say this Miss Baxter of yours did you a favor."

"How do you suppose?"

Harrison's mouth quirked in a half-smile. "Consider this: You have never attempted to sleep in a bed with a woman since the Kitty Newman debacle, correct?" Henry nodded. "But you did sleep with Claudia, didn't you? And nothing bad happened. Nothing bad that *you* instigated, anyway."

"I didn't think of that." Henry rocked back on his heels, his hands deep in his trouser pockets. "But it doesn't change the fact that she orchestrated this whole mess. The whole of Wilmsford-Upon-Avon thinks I'm a degenerate. I don't know how I can ever show my face there again."

Harrison tilted his head. "Don't you?" Henry caught a glimpse of something deep in Harrison's caramel eyes, some knowledge he'd never been able to pinpoint. "You know Claudia Baxter, Henry. You've known her since you were on leading strings. Is she the sort to plot the cruel scheme of which you accuse her?"

Once more peering into the fire, Henry considered Harrison's question. God knew he'd been caught up in plenty of Claudia's schemes over the years. From battle reenactments to new trees to climb to pranks on her governess or his tutor, she'd always had something up her sleeve. "But her games were always meant in fun," he murmured. "She never set out to hurt anyone."

"And you have always been her friend," Harrison pointed out. "From what you've told me, she holds your esteem in as high a regard as that of her twin brother—perhaps higher."

Henry inhaled sharply and looked at Harrison. "Higher? But why …? And if so, then why this abominable stunt?"

Harrison lifted his chin. "What is happening in Claudia's life? There must be something afoot."

Henry exhaled a snort. "Her parents were about to marry her off to a wretched old goat. I put a stop to that."

"Why?"

"Because …" His voice trailed off. Excuses about a potential child and promises made to a woman intoxicated with laudanum crossed his mind, but Henry opted to tell the bald truth. "Because I couldn't bear the thought of her married to another man."

"Does Claudia know about your sleepwalking?"

At this, Henry grimaced. He'd never told her about it, and he'd sworn Claude to secrecy, not wanting to seem diminished in her eyes.

A smile, rueful somehow, crossed Harrison's features. "Don't you see, Henry? Claudia didn't set you up for some sort of sleep-raping witch hunt. She trusts you implicitly. However ill-conceived it may have been, she tried to arrange a scene to get out of an arranged match, and it got away from her. Doesn't that seem more likely than the malicious plot you've imagined?"

Claudia's words from her drug-addled state returned to Henry: *I don't want to marry him. I despise the thought of it. I would be terribly unhappy.* Even the memory of those bleak words caused his heart to lurch. In desperation, she had turned to him. Henry had always played along with her plans in the past; why should she have thought it would be any different this time, in her direst hour, especially if she knew nothing of his somnambulism?

"I do have a question for you." Harrison pulled Henry from his reverie. "You've had your heart set on Miss Baxter all these years. Did you ever once give the woman an inkling of your feelings?"

"No," Henry said defensively. "I knew we couldn't marry, so there was no sense in pursuing her."

Harrison leaned back in his chair, lazily propping one booted foot atop the other. "But you meant to marry her when you thought you'd taken her virtue."

Henry turned and paced in front of the fireplace. "There wasn't any choice, you see?"

"And how, pray tell," Harrison drawled, "did you intend to go about being married to the lovely Miss Baxter, given your vow to never slumber near a woman? Separate chambers?"

"That wouldn't stop me from making a fool of myself. If I started sleepwalking again, I could turn up anywhere."

"Separate residences, then?" The fire caught the white of Harrison's teeth as he gave a teasing grin. "How far do you suppose you could go on foot in your sleep? Perhaps you could set Miss Baxter up one mile beyond your highest estimate—unless, of course, you think you may saddle a horse and ride in search of your bride during an episode, in which case you might have to tuck her away in another county."

In spite of his bleak mood, Henry laughed. Leave it to Harrison to punch holes in his ridiculous ideas.

"And since you aren't actually sleepwalking again, there's no need to resort to such absurd measures," Harrison said, wiping his palms as though settling the matter. "Oh," he frowned, "I forgot. Not only are you not sleepwalking, you didn't actually ravish Miss Baxter, either. I suppose you'll be just as happy letting her get on with marrying her old goat, or some other fellow."

Remembering the way Claudia's supple skin heated beneath his hands on the riverbank, the way her body had become wet and ready for him—for *him*, not for blasted Sir Saint—nearly had Henry running for his horse. When he'd awoken that morning and found her in his bed, everything in Henry's world fell into place. They'd already shared a lifetime of friendship. God (and Claudia) willing, they'd share a lifetime more.

Arms crossed, Henry glowered down at his friend. "I damned well won't just let her marry some other sop."

Harrison gave a small nod. "Well, then, I suppose you have a wife to claim."

Henry sniffed. "I suppose I do."

• • •

As it turned out, Claudia should have asked Claude for a temporal guideline more specific than *soon enough*, because weeks passed with no word from or regarding Henry.

Patience wasn't Claudia's strong suit, but she did try to muster some. The last thing Claude said before leaving for his new life in Somerset had been: *Give him time, Claude. He'll come around.* But it had been two fortnights with nary a sight nor sound of him. And just when she thought she'd mastered a sort of mental tranquility, who should come calling but her erstwhile fiancé?

Sir Saint, too, had been in absentia the past four weeks, thankfully. When he materialized in the doorway of the music room, where Claudia was spending a rainy afternoon half-heartedly practicing the pianoforte, she launched into a funeral dirge. Her fingers plunked out the minor chords in time with his slow progress across the room.

"You might've been a credible governess, my girl, with such skill to recommend you. Good thing I've swooped in to rescue you from such a drear fate, what?"

She accepted his odd compliment with a regal nod. Having avoided her first appointment with the parson's trap, she could spare him a touch of benevolence. Today, he'd left off his musty old satins for a more sober costume of dark blue coat and buff breeches, with a camel waistcoat and white cravat. With a start, she realized he was attempting to imitate the popular dandy style.

It was pathetically touching, in a way, how hard he was trying.

"I'll come straight to the point," he said when she abandoned the death march. "Are you, or are you not, increasing?"

"Heavens!" Claudia bleated. "What a question!"

"I suppose it's my right to know what manner of goods I'm acquiring."

Claudia shot to her feet. "You've no such right! And you aren't acquiring any goods, if by *goods* you mean me."

The old man smirked knowingly, the expression of an aged Lothario unimpressed with her dissembling. "Come now, my dear, you know the score. You're still betrothed to me, which is a sneeze shy of being my wife. Your father insisted on giving you time to nap a kid off De Vere." He rapped the end of his walking stick against the floor to punctuate his speech. "It's been plenty long enough, now, and word has it that scoundrel has scampered off to parts unknown. I wager you're happy to have a constant beau such as m'self, now." He gave her a shrewd look. "So, did you miss your monthly, or not?"

At Claudia's stricken expression, he moderated his tone. "I assure you, it's nothing to me if you have. I don't understand the Puritanical mania that's overcome Society. In my day, we knew better than to wonder aloud where little Johnny got that red hair, when Papa's is black as coal, and Mama's yellow as a canary. Always good to add a little pinch of salt to the pot, I say. Makes the whole dish better, what?"

Mystified by the concept to which Sir Saint had just alluded, Claudia sat with her lips slackened for the space of several seconds.

"Close your mouth, gel," he snapped.

"Sir Saint," she said, rallying her senses to the task at hand, "do you mean to say you harbor no objection to me bearing a child not of your blood?"

"Isn't that what I said?" he demanded hotly. "I'll take a stab, m'self, but as long as you catch, it's nothing to me who throws the seed. The more hands working the field, the better."

Claudia's disgust raised to unprecedented, soaring heights. Her blood boiled so in her cheeks, it was a wonder steam didn't pour from her skin. "Sir Saint, you have just subjected my person to several unflattering comparisons, not to mention the insult you have paid my principles! When I marry, I have no intention of keeping an illicit gentleman friend, and I cannot countenance a husband who would treat the vows of holy matrimony with such blatant disregard!"

Tuggle frowned. "Are you saying you'll not marry me because I'm *too* permissive?"

Whatever does the trick, she decided. "You have it precisely, sir. And now I must bid you a good day, and goodbye forever more."

With a haughty lift of her chin, she flounced into the corridor, where she plowed straight into her mother.

"There you are!" Lady Baxter proclaimed. "You'll never guess what I just heard from Ferguson, who had it from Mr. Airedale, the cheesemonger, who made his delivery to Fairbrook before—"

"Mother!" Claudia interjected, her patience fully eroded by both the irksome guest and the whole trying circumstances of late. "What is it?"

"Henry De Vere is home."

Chapter Ten

It was a lot of commotion that pulled Henry from his hard-earned rest. His eyelids nearly groaned when he forced them open, and his muscles, sore from several long days of travel, protested at being forced upright. His bleary vision struggled to focus in the darkness. It was either still night, or the sun had been extinguished in an apocalyptic catastrophe.

In either case, there was no call for the ruckus coming from elsewhere in the house. There had been a pounding, someone using the iron door knocker over and over, as if to rouse not only Fairbrook's inmates, but also the souls of all those buried within ten miles of the house.

Henry scratched idly at his bare chest, placidly reasoning whatever emergency had brought company at this unholy hour would be dealt with by others. Being the younger son had some advantages, after all.

Around him, the house came to grudging life. Someone from the maids' chambers made her way down the servants' stairs, which passed behind his wall. Meanwhile, the pounding at the door stopped when another someone—a footman, most like—opened it. Voices rose in consternation, a male and a female, engaged in a duet of acrimony.

Henry heard Duncan growl as he stomped past his room. The noise must have roused the elder De Vere, and the midnight exigency almost certainly required the baron's personal attention, in any event. From the entry hall, Duncan's voice bellowed for quiet. Meanwhile, his younger brother relaxed back into his pillows. His jaw creaked in a mighty yawn. Morning would be soon enough to learn the outcome of this drama, before presenting himself at Rudley Court to begin his campaign to win Claudia.

He must have dozed off almost immediately, for he was once more rudely awakened by his door being flung open. Duncan held a candlestick aloft. The flickering light made the features of his face seem to wink in and out of existence above a body wrapped in a thick dressing gown. "You've a caller, Henry." From behind him, he produced a cloaked female.

Claudia, naturally.

"You may have heard the gentle tapping of her summons," Duncan drawled. "Once she'd roused the household, Miss Baxter bullied her way past our brawniest footman, performed an impressive feat of evasive maneuvering to circumvent another footman and a maid, and demanded an audience with you at once. Had I not taken your hellcat into custody, I've no doubt but that she'd have continued menacing the staff. She seemed singularly determined to announce her presence to every body within these walls."

Duncan handed Claudia the candle and nudged her into Henry's room. "The two of you will remain in this chamber until this mess is sorted out. I'm going back to bed. Tomorrow is the Sabbath, and I expect to hear the banns read, or I'll know the reason why." With that he departed, one final slam of the door putting a full stop on the evening's hullabaloo.

There was a moment of awkward silence following Duncan's departure. With one hand, Claudia reached up and released the frog holding her cloak closed at her neck. Henry knew a second of anticipation, watching the heavy garment slide down her back to the floor. Beneath it, she wore one of her simple dresses and sensible half-boots. He didn't know what else he'd have expected, but it wasn't such a perfectly ordinary-looking Claudia to show up in his room at—

"What's the bloody time?" he inquired.

She used the candle to light several others, filling the room with a cozy glow. "About half-one." When she finished lighting the candles, she helped herself to a drink from the glass of water on his bedside table.

Lowering to a chair facing the bed, Claudia unlaced her boots, removed them, then raised her skirts to untie her garters and roll down her stockings. Every inch of exposed, creamy skin raised his level of alarm, as well as his heart rate.

"What are you doing?" he demanded. "Everyone in the house knows you're in my room. You can't do this. You must go."

The smile on her lips seemed different from those he'd had from Claudia in the past. It was a touch winsome, a touch mischievous, but there was something new and secret there, too, something knowing and fully feminine.

Without a word, Claudia continued shedding her attire. She was far too innocent to know the art of undressing for a man's appreciation. Claudia went about disrobing in a straightforward fashion, neatly folding her garments and piling them on the clothespress as she went. And it drove him wilder than any contrived seduction could ever hope to do. He was hard before she'd shucked her chemise. She unpinned her hair, allowing a single, heavy braid to fall over her left shoulder. On silent feet, she came to the side of the bed, naked.

Henry threw back the covers and rose to meet her. He grabbed her arms, simultaneously longing to hold her close and pitch her out the door. The weeks of his absence should have been time enough to get his thoughts in order, but they hadn't been. Anger and hurt and lust and longing all roiled through his gut. And even though his conversation with Harrison had helped him put his mind in order, Henry had thought he'd have the benefit of a respectable hour before having to carry out a conversation with her.

"Claudia, why are you here?" he asked.

She blinked up at him, her eyes round and trusting. "I've come to do this." She slipped from his grasp and fell to her knees before him, her eyes level with his erection.

Merciful God. It was another Claudia dream. He was going to spend in his sleep and wake, alone, with a mess on his stomach.

But his dream took an unexpected turn when Claudia clasped her hands together at her chest and gazed up pleadingly.

"Henry De Vere, I've come to offer my sincere apology. I'm so sorry for the trick I played with the pig's blood. It was beastly selfish and I—"

He took her hands and hauled her to her feet. "Sweetheart, I can't hear a word you say in that position."

Not that this was much better. She was fantastically, gorgeously naked. Her breasts, full and firm, begged for his mouth like the most succulent pears. And then, suddenly, she was in his arms. His hands circled her waist and pulled her against him as she threw her arms around his neck. Oh, she was a warm and delightful woman. His cock brushed against the soft brown curls on her mound—death by intimate tickling.

She trembled in his embrace. "I'm so sorry, Henry," she said, her voice thick with unshed tears.

As angry as he'd been, he still couldn't stand to see her in pain. "Hush now," he murmured. One hand stroked her back, the other cradled her head to his torso, then worked into her hair and rubbed her scalp.

Claudia's hand came to rest on his chest beside her face. Her fingers curled; her nails grazed lightly across his skin. "No, please let me speak, Henry. I'll never be able to look myself in the mirror again if I do not get this out."

"Go on, then."

"I was desperate not to marry Sir Saint."

"I know, lamb."

"But I couldn't see any way out of it. Then you came that day, and I had the idea." By the shift in her tone and the hitch of her breath, he knew tears had started falling. With the backs of his fingers, he lightly brushed the moisture from her cheek.

"I wasn't trying to be cruel to you. I swear I didn't know you or anyone else would think you'd abused me. I would never, *never* want anyone to think ill of you. I just ... I hoped if I made them believe I was ruined, then I wouldn't have to marry him. But, Henry?" She lifted her head to look up at him.

"What, love?"

"Deep down, what I really believed—what I *knew*—was that if I could just make it to you, everything would be all right. You would make sure of it. I just ... I just had to get to you." She cradled the sides of his face; her thumbs brushed back and forth over his cheeks. "But it had to be you. I love you, you see, and I—"

Her confession was so damn sweet, it made his heart ache. He sealed his mouth on hers, needing a moment to absorb what she'd said. To think, all the while he'd wanted her so badly, she'd been wanting him, too. It was heady stuff, enough to make a man want to start making up for those weeks of lost time. Softly, he probed with his tongue at the seam of her mouth. She sighed and opened, sliding her tongue against his.

After a few minutes of luxuriously slow, drugging kisses, Henry started down the slender column of her neck. Lips and tongue worked in tandem to locate her pulse. He was delighted to feel her heartbeat quicken beneath her delicate skin.

"I never would have had the courage to climb into that bed with anyone else," she said in a sleepy voice.

Henry grunted. "Damn right. You're mine, Claudia, do you hear me?"

She sighed something that sounded like acquiescence, but it might have been in response to the brush of his fingers over the crease where her lush fundament met silky thighs. His hands stilled. "Claudia?"

"Hmm?" Slowly, she opened her eyes, dreamy and unfocused. "I love you."

Her gaze sharpened. "Oh!" She pressed the back of her hand against her mouth.

"I want to marry you. Not because of Sir Saint, or because you've ruined me and I've ruined you—although we *have* thoroughly ruined one another," he said with a lopsided grin, "especially with your midnight storming of the walls. By breakfast, the whole village will know about this."

She exhaled a teary laugh. "My diabolical scheme is revealed."

He smiled and tucked an errant strand of her hair behind one ear, gazing at her with all the emotion he'd longed to express for years now. "But because I need you," he continued. "I was devastated when I thought I'd hurt you, Claudia. You're the last person I would ever wish to harm. And I'm sorry I lashed back. Leaving you beside the river as I did …" He swallowed around a lump of guilt.

She shook her head. "No, don't. What you did was just. You gave me much to think on. Besides …" Her hip pressed against his groin. His breath hitched at the sharp pang of desire. "I didn't stop you, did I? I was willing. I wanted you. I want you."

Hot blood thundered through his veins. If he had any chance of finishing his proposal in a coherent fashion, he had to get on with the business. He took a half-step back and pressed on. "When I was a boy, it was you, Claudia, who made me feel part of the family at Rudley Court. It was you whose company I craved, whose mind I couldn't wait to engage. All these years, Claude has been like a brother, but you were *never* a sister. You were always different, always more. You were always … mine."

He took Claudia's right hand in both of his own and dropped to one knee. The view from here was agonizing. The softly rounded skin of her belly was flushed a pale pink. Inviting warmth emanated from her body, and—God above—he could smell her arousal. *WANT,* his body announced. His balls were heavy and tight. Panting, he swayed and placed a kiss right below her navel. Her stomach twitched. He smiled against her.

"Claudia Baxter," he said, "will you do me the very great honor of marrying me?"

For a small eternity, she just stared at him with huge, doe eyes and her bottom lip crushed between her teeth.

Henry's body, meanwhile, vibrated like the strings inside a pianoforte being hammered away at by a cantankerous toddler. His arousal had become painful, all anticipation with no relief in sight. He worried his mind might snap, that he might, in fevered desperation, mount her leg, like his mother's dastardly little terrier.

"Claudia, you're killing me," he stated. "If you aren't ready to answer, all right, but I'll need to excuse myself for a few—"

"Yes," she said. Then her arms were around his head and neck, pressing his face into her abdomen. "Oh, yes, yes, yes, Henry! *Yes!*"

A man could only take so much, Henry reasoned, and when his new (and naked) fiancée wrapped her arms about him and called out his name and that breathy little *Yes!* he reached his limit. He swept her up suddenly, turned around, and deposited her in the middle of the bed.

And then he lowered his mouth to her pinked, slick flesh and kissed her.

Claudia yelped and twisted. Henry gave her a swat on the rump. "Be still," he growled against her nether lips.

"What are you doing?" she demanded. "That can't be seemly."

"But swiving you by the river would have been?"

"Swiving? Is that what you call this?"

"Not really, no." The tip of his tongue dragged circles around her small button. Claudia's moans and mewls were addictive. He wanted to hear the next one, and the next; he would do whatever it took to bring those sounds of pleasure to her lips. Two fingers gently parted her folds. He lapped at her entrance, savoring the smell and taste of her.

Claudia's hands scrabbled in his hair and slapped the bed. "That's … that's … oh!"

With one hand, he reached up and covered a breast, palming the firm roundness while his mouth continued its sensual assault. His other thumb rubbed lightly across her clitoris.

"Henry!" she cried.

"Is this too much?" His voice rumbled against her sex. "Shall I stop?"

Claudia stilled. "Don't you dare," she panted. "Please, keep swiving me."

He chuckled. "I told you," he drawled between long laps along her slick length, "this isn't swiving."

"What's swiving, then?" She sounded breathless and bewildered.

Henry propped up on an elbow. Claudia's face was flushed. Strands of hair, worked loose from her braid, frizzled around her head. "Swiving, my dearest Miss Baxter, is when I enter your body with my own, when we bring each other to pleasure and completion." Her mouth dropped open in an adorable O. "Swiving," and now he was kissing his way back down her belly, "is when I drive into you over and over." One finger pressed into her tight entrance—just a bit—to offer a practical demonstration. "You'll wrap your legs around my hips and beg me to go faster or harder or slower." The erotic words provoked himself as much as her. His hips rolled against the bed, but he found no ease on the linen sheets. Instead, he only succeeded in ratcheting his torment up another notch. He drew her swollen nub into his mouth and sucked, long and slow. Claudia arched off the bed and made a keening sound. "And I'll tease you and love you until we come apart in each others' arms, sweetheart." He sucked on her again. And again. And one more time.

And then her hot flesh rippled around his finger and bathed him in her sweet nectar. An inarticulate cry slid into a groan. As the shudders of her climax ebbed, Henry pressed up on his knees. It would be the easiest thing in the world to slide home into her welcoming body. It seemed the natural thing to do. He wanted her so damn much.

But.

Something of his dilemma must have shown on his face. Claudia cooed. She wound her arms around his neck and brought him down for a kiss—on the mouth this time. "Thank you," she whispered. "That was the most glorious thing I've ever felt." Her legs, limber with repletion, slid up his sides. Her feet caressed the backs of his calves. The head of his cock brushed against her wet heat. He hissed.

"Do it, Henry," she urged, all earnestness. "Swive me."

A snort erupted from his throat. He laughed and shifted off of her, flopping on his back at her side. A look of consternation crossed her face. "What's the matter? Don't you want to?"

As if to speak for itself, his throbbing cock twitched. Henry took himself in hand. "Oh, I want to, sweetheart. But for all that we're ruined, I won't take your maidenhead before we're wed." Her brow puckered. He drew his hand up his shaft. "Just look, Claudia. This is how much I want you."

Shyly, her gaze tracked down his body. Her nostrils flared at the sight of his engorged member. A small hand tentatively reached toward him. "May I?" she asked.

"God, yes," he blurted.

One fingertip perched lightly on the tip. She drew the bead of moisture there down his thick length. Henry's breath stuttered in his throat. Sweat beaded on his forehead. He gritted his teeth, determined not to erupt at a single touch of his lady's finger. As she brought her hand around, gripping him in imitation of his example, he started counting backwards from five hundred, by sevens.

Her silky palm glided upward. "Is this right?"

He clamped his hand over hers. "Tighter, like this."

"I don't want to hurt you," she protested.

He chuckled. "You won't. He's a sturdy little beggar." Henry showed Claudia the pace he wanted. After a few strokes, his hips involuntarily bucked. "That's it," he rasped. "Just like that."

Claudia seemed to really get into the spirit of the thing; she nudged his hand away and took charge.

Henry wrapped her braid around his wrist and pulled her head to him. He kissed her savagely, plundering her mouth as he could not yet her body. His buttocks clenched and his balls drew tight. Warm fluid spurted onto his belly while waves of intense pleasure racked his body.

Claudia made a little sound of alarm. As he came down from his euphoria, Henry peeked out from under heavy eyelids, dreading to see her disgust of his body's response.

Instead, she was regarding the mess with seeming interest. "Everything all right?" he asked, cautious.

Claudia dragged a finger through his seed. "I just wish … This should have happened inside me, shouldn't it have?"

Henry gathered her into his arms. "I love you," he murmured.

She nuzzled against his neck. "I love you, too, Henry."

Later, after he cleaned them with a wet flannel and extinguished the candles, Henry drew Claudia's back against his chest. She fit just right in his arms, her bottom snug against his groin and her head right beneath his chin. And for a virgin, she took awfully well to falling asleep, naked, in a man's arms. Which reminded him …

"Claudia?" he asked, his voice thick with the sleep creeping over him.

"Hmm?"

"Why did you take off your clothes when you came into my room?"

"Because," she said, her voice likewise drifting out to the sea of dreams, "I needed you to see me for who I honestly am. No tricks, no lies." Her voice floated away, and he thought she'd gone to sleep, when she suddenly spoke again. "Besides, when I'm alone with you, taking off my clothes feels like the right thing to do. It's all right?"

He smiled into her hair. "Yes, darling. It's all right."

Epilogue

Marriage to Henry, Claudia thought, was a marvelous state in which to find herself. After her impromptu trip to Fairbrook led to that second scandalous night spent with Henry, there was no question but that they would have to wed. Together, they faced her parents' chastisement. Henry held her hand when they told the vicar of Claudia's change in prospective bridegroom. From Duncan, there was only a sigh of relief, followed by a brotherly kiss on her cheek, welcoming Claudia to the family.

The village was all abuzz with gossip, but in true Claudia fashion, she simply put a smile on her face and brazened it out. There was some brief talk of a special license, but Claudia put an end to that codswallop. It wouldn't do, she said, to act furtive and ashamed. Besides, she couldn't possibly marry without Claude present. Everyone who mattered understood that, at least.

And so Claudia spent two months as an engaged lady, during which time Henry was fastidious in courting her properly. There were rides and drives and promenades, but no more glorious nights like the one they'd spent at Fairbrook. Whenever Claudia's kisses became a little too urgent, or her hands a little too bold, Henry set her aside with a smile which, over time, became ever more strained.

The day of her wedding began with rain, but cleared to a beautiful, late summer day. The earth and everything on it looked that much nicer, she decided, for the fresh washing. Her father escorted her to the front of the little church and placed her hand in Henry's. On her other side, Claude grinned and gave her a wink of encouragement. Henry had griped about Claudia poaching his best man, but Claudia pointed out twindom gave her greater claim to her brother's services as attendant. Besides, Henry had

The Honorables in attendance, who had all embraced Claudia like a long-lost sister. Lorna Dewhurst claimed to be ecstatic to have another woman in the group, and Claudia already liked her immensely. Harrison Dyer stood with Henry, his keen gaze assessing Claudia and, thankfully, finding her worthy of his friend.

After hours of feasting and fêting and dancing until she'd nearly worn a hole in her new slippers, Claudia and Henry departed Rudley Court and made the short drive to Fairbrook, where Duncan did them the very great honor of making no appearance whatsoever. In fact, he and his mother, along with The Honorables, were ensconced at Rudley Court for the next several days, even though the newlyweds planned to take up immediate residence in Fairbrook's dower house.

There were more felicitations from the footman and maid at the dower house, and proclamations of delight over the supper *à deux* which had been laid out for them, and compliments to be conveyed to the chef in the main house and then finally, *finally*, Henry politely booted the servants out the door and whisked his wife to bed.

And as he'd promised, Henry teased her and loved her so thoroughly and well, that when, at last, he pushed his body into her own, there was only a brief discomfort, like a hard pinch. He held himself still for a while, allowing her time to adjust to the new sensation. After a moment, the pain passed and Claudia became restless. Her legs hooked around his hips; her hands held him tight to her chest. She arched against him and made a wordless plea for ... something.

Henry withdrew and surged forward, filling her completely. His long, deep strokes caressed her insides with the most loving, intimate touch imaginable. Pressure built in her womb. Henry butted against the entrance of it over and over, while his mouth and hands showered attention on her lips, her breasts, her throat.

This, Claudia decided, was swiving.

Then came the stroke that ruptured the pressure inside her and flung it through her body in a surge of exquisite pleasure. "Henry," she heard herself cry, as if from a distance. And her heart was so full, so blessedly complete, she could not help but add, "I love you so much."

Henry gripped her hair in a fist. "Love you, too," he rasped, still pumping deep, harder and faster now. With every thrust, his skin slapped against that swollen bud at the apex of her thighs. "Again, Claudia. Come with me."

And her body responded to his demand. Her feet planted and her lower back arched to meet him while the pleasure was wrenched from her gut. This climax was deeper. Hotter. A rush of sensation stoppered her ears and eyes and even her scalp tingled. Henry gripped her hips hard. A savage yell tore from his throat while he throbbed inside her. The hot pulse of his seed added another layer to her satisfaction.

"God!" he bellowed, his hips pressing her into the bed. His chest was slick with sweat and heaved against hers. He lay heavily on top of her for a while, until, at last, he withdrew from her body and stretched out beside her. Their legs and fingers tangled together in a sweaty heap of repletion.

In her husband's arms, Claudia lazed. They spoke quietly and laughed and kissed and dozed. It was so natural, so right, to be with Henry. Running to his guest room that fateful night, she thought, a little smugly, was the best thing she'd ever done.

"Oh!" she exclaimed.

"What?" Henry asked. His hand followed as she sat up in bed; his fingers lazily sifted through her hair.

Without answering, Claudia scooted over and pulled back the sheets. She gasped. Tears of guilt and humiliation filled her eyes.

Henry glanced at the unimpressive little pink smear and raised a brow. "Your interpretation was much more dramatic. No wonder they all thought I'd tried to bludgeon you to death with my cock."

A laugh burst from her lips. Henry drew her back down into his arms and kissed her soundly. "No more apologies, Claudia. You've ruined me, and now you'll just have to make the best of it."

Happiness swept away the last cobwebs of sadness. She curled against her husband and set about making the best of it with him.

Over and over again.

The End

About the Author

Elizabeth Boyce is an aficionado of the British Regency, rooftop pools, and Cumberbatch. She's the bestselling author of the Once trilogy, The Honorables series, and many sternly-worded emails to her elected officials. She lives in South Carolina with a gaggle of people who share her last name.

Keep up with Elizabeth!
  Blog: *http://bluestockingball.blogspot.com/*
  Facebook: *https://www.facebook.com/AuthorElizabethBoyce*
  Twitter: @EBoyceRomance

More from This Author
(From *Honor Among Thieves* by Elizabeth Boyce)

1816, Middlesex

The grandfather clock in the corner thunked a steady rhythm, and Lorna sipped her tea. Around her, the parlor's shabby sofa and chairs stood empty, waiting for callers who wouldn't arrive. No one mourned the passing of a madman.

A series of hollow gongs announced ten o'clock. At the cemetery, the vicar soon would pray over Thomas, with only poor little Daniel and a manservant in attendance.

The droning chimes faded. Silence filled Lorna's ears, a soothing balm to her frayed nerves. Her brother's screams and curses had filled the house for months before the end came. Belligerent and wheedling and sinister by turns, the incessant noise had threatened to pull the whole house into insanity with him. Even when he no longer opened his lids because light hurt his eyes, his lips moved, spewing blasphemies and mad rants or begging for something— the services of a prostitute his most frequent request.

On one of these occasions, her resolve to ignore his revolting words had failed her. "Hasn't your whoring done enough?" she'd snapped. "There will be no more of that for you, brother."

Thomas growled in protest and squirmed against the lengths of linen bound to his ankles and wrists. One eye cracked open, rolling in the socket until it settled on Lorna. It looked like a watery poached egg floating in a ring of crusty lashes. Gaunt, stubbled cheeks pulled back to reveal slimy teeth. "Then give me *your* mouth." The thin, soiled nightshirt wadded around his thighs outlined a jutting erection.

Lorna's cheeks still burned in shame to recall her brother's suggestion. He'd laughed at her shocked indignation, all the while lewdly grinding his hips in circles. "You're too scrawny to fuck, and your cunt's dusty like a harp in the corner, waiting for someone to play it. But your lips are pink and ready." She'd never heard two of those words before, but it took her only a second to interpret them.

Lorna took a cake from the table of refreshments meant for sympathetic neighbors. Cook insisted on providing the late Baron Chorley a respectable funeral, despite the disgrace he had heaped upon the family while he lived. Lorna nibbled slowly, relishing the sweetness against her tongue.

Of late, her meals had been gulped down without tasting the food. Almost every waking moment had been spent at Thomas's bedside, watching the restraints. Twice he'd escaped. The first time, he kicked through a window, shredded his leg, and nearly bled to death before they wrestled him back into bed. The second time … Lorna winced at the memory of the maid's ruined face.

After that, Thomas was kept under constant supervision. Lorna hadn't thought it fair to leave the last remaining footman, Oscar, and the old butler, Humphrey, entirely in charge of tending him— especially since the servants worked out of loyalty now, rather than for a decent wage.

Lorna swept a few crumbs from the skirt of her black dress. The garment began its life a pale rose, but the necessity for mourning weeds had seen it dunked into a stinking vat of vinegar and dye just yesterday. Mrs. Lynch, the housekeeper, had smoothed an old sheet over Lorna's chair before she sat, lest dye bleed onto the faded upholstery.

A knock sounded at the front door. Lorna set down her teacup and folded her hands in her lap a few seconds before Humphrey's stooped form appeared in the parlor door. "A Mr. Wiggins is here, Miss Robbins," he said, presenting the caller's card.

"Show him in," she said.

The name sparked no recognition, but Lorna did not know most of Thomas's acquaintance. Fifteen years her senior, her half-brother had been mostly absent from Lorna's life. She'd made rare, brief visits to London, and he came home with even less frequency, despite the family seat being only a handful of miles outside of Town. They'd spent no length of time together until six months ago, when one of his London companions unceremoniously dumped him, soaking wet and raving, on the portico. From what Lorna had been able to piece together, Thomas had no friends, only people to whom he was indebted. If this Mr. Wiggins had come from Town to pay his respects, though, perhaps he'd been a true friend to her brother.

Humphrey returned with her guest. The man was not much taller than she, several inches over five feet. Stringy gray hair inadequately covered a balding pate, and the man's middle paunch had a sadly deflated quality to it, like an empty wineskin. His apparel looked fine at a distance, but when he took her hand in greeting, Lorna noted frayed cuffs and thin places at the seams. *Not that I've room to judge,* she thought, glancing at her own tatty furnishings.

"Miss Robbins," he said, "please accept my condolences for your loss." His accent carried the remnants of a working class upbringing.

"Thank you, Mr. Wiggins." Lorna took her seat and gestured him to a chair. "May I offer you some tea?"

"With my gratitude." As Lorna handed him a cup, he said, "I was hoping I might see Lord Chorley."

"Oh." Lorna faltered, grasping for delicate words. "I'm afraid that won't be possible. The viewing has ended. My brother has been moved to the church for burial. Unless ..." She twisted her fingers together, uncertain about the protocol of graveside services. "If you hurry to the churchyard, you might be able to see him before … But I really don't know."

Wiggins gulped his beverage and smacked his lips. "I'll wait," he announced. "I've got no pressing engagements."

Lorna frowned. "I'm sorry, sir. Do you mean you wish to see the new Lord Chorley, not the deceased?"

"Just so," Wiggins replied. "I've no wish to peep at a soul case." His eyes narrowed on Lorna in suspicion. "Unless this is another ruse to get out of paying his notes. Has he skipped to Calais?"

Lorna suppressed a groan. So Mr. Wiggins wasn't a friend, after all. "If it's money you're after, sir, I'm afraid I cannot help you."

The man nodded. "Then we're all right, miss. I wouldn't dream of treating with a lady, so if you don't mind passing me one of those cakes, I'll just await his lordship's return."

One of her cakes, indeed. Lorna raised her chin a notch. "You mistake me, Mr. Wiggins. I run this household, not his lordship. Any understanding between you and my late brother is none of my affair, and I refuse to be drawn into his financial mishaps." She stood, calling upon every ounce of her girlhood comportment training to maintain a polite tone. "I do thank you for your condolences, Mr. Wiggins, but I'm afraid I must bid you a good day."

Wiggins wagged a knobby finger. "Now, now, missy, that dodge will never hold up in a court of law." From a pocket he produced a stack of notes, which he handed to Lorna.

A cursory examination showed amounts to make her stomach clench. A hundred pounds. Fifty. Five hundred twenty. All carried her worthless brother's signature, all dated within the last eighteen months. "Thomas was … sick," she said, her throat catching around the allusion to his insanity, "when he borrowed from you."

Wiggins sneered, all pretense of politeness dropped. "He's not the first taken by the French disease, and he won't be the last, but I'm out the coin anyway. My business is with Chorley. If the baron I knew has escaped to hell, then I'll speak to the new man in charge. He'll make good on these notes, all right, or I'll have the law on him."

The threat against Daniel turned Lorna's despair to rage in an instant. "*The new man in charge*," she said, venom dripping from her words, "is a boy of seven. You cannot hold him responsible for another's debts." She threw the stack of notes right back in Wiggins's face, where they exploded like confetti.

A shadow darkened the moneylender's features an instant before he chuckled. He reclined in the chair, more at his ease than when she'd offered him tea and pleasantries. "Oh, but I can. Lord Chorley is responsible, and it doesn't matter a whit to me if he's a babe in arms. I'll bring suit against the estate. It'll cost you dear to have a barrister speak for you, and you'll still have to pay up in the end."

She closed her eyes and scratched at her head with both hands, an anxious habit she'd abandoned years ago—until Thomas came home. Now thin weals crisscrossed her scalp. She winced as her nails dragged across them; the pain brought clarity. Lorna rounded on him. A faint smell of vinegar wafted from her skirts as they swished around her legs. "All right, Wiggins, look." If he could drop the social façade, so could she. "I have perhaps twenty pounds to my name. Take it or leave it." She looked down her nose, raising a brow in challenge.

He guffawed.

"Twenty pounds, the chit says!" He wheezed through a laugh, his face going puce with the force of his amusement. "If that's not the best demmed jape I've heard this age and more." He wiped tears from his cheeks with the ratty cuff of his coat. Then he gathered up the promissory notes and tucked them into his pocket. "I'll leave your twenty and take the fifteen hun'ret I'm owed, miss."

He smiled as he rose to his feet, but the malice gleaming in his eyes sent ice to Lorna's toes. Wiggins stepped toward her. Lorna instinctively retreated. "I will have my due. Need be, I'll take this house and everything in it; I happen to know it ain't entailed. Better for you to sell on your terms, than give it to me on mine. You have two months, then it's pay up or else."

Sell Elmwood? Everything inside of Lorna rebelled at the notion. For years, she had worked to keep the estate's ledgers balanced. She had scrimped and cut back and done without, all to provide Daniel a safe, happy home. Thomas never did anything for his half-siblings. He couldn't be bothered to visit the small property more than once every few years. No, it had been Lorna's duty to keep everything running. And now Thomas was threatening to ruin her carefully ordered world from beyond the grave. She wouldn't allow it.

"Absolutely not," she declared. "I won't give up my home."

"Then you'll have to cough up the blunt some other way." Wiggins gave her an appraising look. "Might be you've something else to sell."

Lorna took leave to doubt that.

In response to her dubious expression, Wiggins turned cajoling. "You *could* use some meat on those bones, but there's some as like the skinny ones. Not to mention being the first to breach the walls, as it were, commands a higher rate—"

She shoved him, hard, toward the door. He stumbled and cracked his shin against a side table. The impact drew a hiss of pain from Wiggins.

"Get out," Lorna said in a low voice. "Take your notes and your filthy mouth, and get out of my house."

Wiggins rubbed his injury through his pant leg. "You're gonna wish you hadn't done that. I'll be back. Fifteen hundred. Cough it up, or I'll choke it from you." The moneylender limped from the room.

An hour later, Daniel found her. His dark eyes were wide and solemn in his slender face. Oscar the footman patted the new baron on the shoulder before leaving him in Lorna's care. When they were alone, Daniel curled up beside her, heedless of his formal black suit. Her arms twined around her young half-brother, pulling him into her lap, where he nestled against her. He was getting too big to fit comfortably, but neither of them was ready to give up the familiar closeness.

While Lorna had a few scant memories of her own mother, Daniel had none of his. His mother, their father's third wife, had died only hours after his birth. Following her burial, their father took a drunken ride. Never much of a horseman in the best of times, he was thrown from the saddle and broke his neck. At the age of fourteen, Lorna became the only parent Daniel had ever known.

She pressed her hands to the boy's face. "Your cheeks are cold, darling," Lorna murmured, lightly rubbing the pink skin to warm him.

"Yours are wet, Sissy." Daniel's chilled fingers smeared a tear toward her ear. His pale features pinched together. "Are you crying because you miss Brother?"

Lorna gave a watery laugh. As if she could miss the wastrel who had only brought them ruin. "No, sweetling, I'm crying because I missed *you*."

His slim arms circled her neck. "It's a silly rule, that ladies can't go to a burial. Now that I'm baron, I'm going to change it. You should be able to do anything you please."

She nuzzled the top of his head. His hair, honey-tinged brown, smelled of wind and dry leaves. "My own little knight in egalitarian armor." Fierce love thundered through her body. She would protect Daniel from Mr. Wiggins and anyone else who threatened her family. No matter what, she would keep Daniel safe and give him a home.

Even if she had to sell herself, body and soul, to do it.

• • •

After tucking Daniel into bed, Lorna swathed herself in Thomas's billowing black cloak and stepped outside. The early November evening carried a bite in the air, but she welcomed the brisk chill.

Her sturdy boots carried her across the lawn and down the familiar path through the small home wood to the lane heading into the village. The gathering dusk didn't signify. Her feet knew every root and stone along the way.

Since the funeral, Lorna had kept a semblance of calm about her for Daniel's sake. After the harrowing months they'd endured, the boy needed a return to the order of their life before Thomas's illness. All through the day, though, anger built inside her, until she felt her ribs would crack with it. The fire in her belly drove her onward.

Avoiding the village high street, Lorna slipped down the alley beside a tavern. Yellow light and sounds of male conversation seeped from chinks between the boards. She shrank from the light and noise, clinging to the shadows.

Two turnings brought her to the church, and a quick sprint across dead grass took her to her brother's grave. A little nosegay Lorna gave Daniel for the purpose lay atop the mound of earth. Thomas had a place in consecrated ground, blessed with the peace he'd ripped away from her.

Rage bubbled up from her gut, filling her throat and choking her. She wanted to scream at Thomas, to lash out at him for destroying the home she'd worked so hard to keep. How was she to find the money to pay the wretched Wiggins, except to sell her home or herself? A terrible choice. An impossible one. Marriage wasn't even a viable option. Lorna had no suitors. No man came sniffing after the homely daughter of a poor, country baron. Even if she started hunting a husband now, she would never marry in time to save Elmwood from Wiggins. No hero would swoop in to deliver them from ruin—it was up to Lorna to protect her family. She wished she knew the vile words Thomas knew. Nothing in her feeble lady's vocabulary was profane enough to express her outrage.

But she did know a couple, she recalled, compliments of her dear brother.

"Cunt." The word felt guttural, like a good, cleansing cough. "Fuck." Lorna didn't know how to use them in a sentence, but they were the worst words she'd ever heard. She hurled them at her dead sibling repeatedly, imbuing them with a healthy dose of hatred. When she'd had her fill of obscenities, she spat on his grave, in defiance of God's law and man's.

"How could you do this to us?" she demanded of her sibling. The anger that had sustained her all day turned to apprehension. "What shall I do?"

The more Lorna considered the hopelessness of her situation, the more she felt herself swamped by dread. Suddenly, her chest seized; her lungs refused to draw air. Fear clawed at her throat. *Have to get away.* Escape was the only thought left to her. If she stayed in this spot, she would surely die. Some distant part of her mind recognized no immediate threat, but the larger portion of Lorna's consciousness was overcome with the certainty of impending doom.

She whirled in a billow of black wool and launched herself into a dead run, her skin crackling as if from an imminent lightning strike. Lorna's feet only carried her a short distance from Thomas's resting place before she fell to her knees. Her vision narrowed and her ears rang, and then she knew no more.

Some time later, Lorna awakened to darkness. Her eyes felt gritty and her head ached, after-effects of the terrifying episode she'd suffered. She was in the cemetery, she recalled, curled inside

Thomas's cloak. She pulled it from her face and choked back a yelp.

A huge hound loomed over her, slobber dangling in twin strands from loose jowls. It pressed a cold nose into her neck and snuffled. Lorna shoved at the beast's head. "Get off," she hissed. The dog licked her face.

"Hey, wassat?" The voice was nearby. "Coop," it called in a whisper. "Bluebell found somethin'."

"Body?" answered another voice—Coop, Lorna surmised. "S'not like the digger to leave one out. Might be one for the pauper pit. Pretty Lem, see what's what."

Lorna tried to back out from under the slavering Bluebell, but her hairy captor simply flopped down on her chest, pinning her. A few seconds later, a figure appeared with a shuttered lantern, illuminating the tan and black bloodhound. "Good girl, Blue. What you got? Is it—oh, shit!"

Lorna just made out the surprised face of a young man before he ran in the other direction. Bluebell heaved herself up and loped after Pretty Lem. "It's a lady, Coop! A live one! Pack it up, boys."

"Can't yet," said Coop. "Bob's in the ground."

Lorna scrambled behind a nearby gravestone. When no one immediately pounced on her, she peeked over the top. It was still night, dark except for the light of two lanterns illuminating a group of four men. They wore roughspun clothes, with scarves, gloves, and hats shielding them from the cold. Pretty Lem frantically gestured to where he'd found Lorna. One tall, lanky man propped himself against a shovel driven into the ground, as casual as you please. A third stood at the light's edge, minding a mule team hitched to a wagon. The fourth man, average in height and build, exuded an air of authority. He had to be Coop, the leader. That one listened to Pretty Lem and peered into the darkness. Lorna ducked behind the stone.

"Fartleberry, the second we've got the goods, start filling. Lem, you and me'll load." Coop issued orders with military efficiency. "Out o' the earth bath, Bob."

Bob's in the ground, he'd said a moment ago. The hair on her nape stood on end as she peered once more over the gravestone. An elongated, white shape emerged from the dank ground. In a sickening rush, Lorna realized they had opened her brother's grave.

Before she could consider the folly of it, she was pounding toward the gang. "Stop!" she cried. The too-large cloak tangled around her legs; she went sprawling, face first, into the loose soil that used to cover her brother.

The gangmen glanced her way, but continued their grisly work. Coop dragged Thomas's wrapped body away from the grave, while the thug he'd called Fartleberry gave a hand to a fifth man emerging from the ground.

Lorna sputtered dirt and swiped at her nose. She'd spat on Thomas's grave just hours before, and thought it the worst insult possible. Compared to this atrocity, it seemed a tender caress. "Put him back!" she demanded.

The hulking brute fresh from the ground leaped the open hole and grabbed Lorna around the middle. He hauled her away from the dirt, which Fartleberry began shoveling back into Thomas's empty grave.

"What'll we do wif her, Coop?" the big man's voice rumbled.

Fartleberry chucked dirt into the hole at an impressive rate. Lorna noted the shovel the man used had a wooden head, not iron. "We oughter do her and sell three, 'stead of two." His words were muffled by the scarf covering the bottom half of his face. The calm way he suggested Lorna's demise made her lightheaded.

"We're not doing nobody," Coop said.

He and Pretty Lem loaded Thomas into the back of the wagon, alongside another corpse. Bluebell propped her front feet on the wagon bed and sniffed the bodies, while Lem retrieved another shovel and joined his comrade in moving dirt.

"Ten quid ain't worth our necks." Coop wiped his hands on his baggy trousers, then swatted Fartleberry on the back of the head. "Use your breadbox 'fore you go spouting off, fool."

He sauntered toward Lorna with a lantern. She twisted in her big captor's hands. For her pains, Bob merely lifted her from the ground and held her more securely against his filthy coat. He smelled of death and worms. Her head swam.

Coop hoisted the lantern to her face. Lorna squinted at the light. "You picked the wrong night for a midnight stroll, girl."

As her eyes adjusted, Lorna took in details. Coop had a large nose, spiderwebbed with blood vessels. His ruddy cheeks were covered in gray stubble. Pale, suspicious eyes squinted at her.

"I wasn't strolling," Lorna informed him, "I was visiting my brother's grave." She kicked her boot heel into the big man's shin, earning an "Oi!" in return. "Tell your ruffian to let me go."

"Set 'er down, Bob, but keep a hand on 'er."

As soon as Lorna's feet touched the ground, she ducked out of Bob's grasp and darted to the wagon. She tugged at the dingy linen covering her brother. "Put him back! He isn't wearing any valuables, nothing worth stealing."

Bob reached her in a few quick strides and snatched her arms. Bluebell bayed and pranced around them in a circle, as if they were playing a game.

"Beggin' to differ, miss, but we got what we came for." Coop's nose dripped; he swiped it with the fringe of his scarf. "Daft Jemmy," he called to the mule handler, "get the team ready to go." To the men filling Thomas's grave, he said, "Double time, lads. We're gone in five. Harty Choke Boys won't be none pleased when they find we've picked their garden."

Fartleberry grunted in reply. He wielded his shovel like a fencing master with a foil, graceful and swift. The hole was nearly full again. Beside him, Pretty Lem methodically arranged the soil neatly at the edges so it resembled the undertaker's original work.

"What do you mean, you've got what you came for?" Lorna demanded. "Who's the other body? And why do you want them? Thomas wasn't important. He wasn't …"

She trailed off as Coop chuckled. Behind him, Pretty Lem gently replaced Daniel's nosegay atop of the grave. Once the gang cleared out, no one would ever know tonight's macabre crime had taken place. No one but Lorna.

From the wagon bed, Coop fetched a coil of rope. "Your Tommy might not've been worth anything to you," he said as he approached, "but he's worth ten quid to the anatomists. Maybe twelve, if we can offload 'im fresh."

The implication shocked Lorna to her core. She barely noticed as Bob spun her so Coop could tie her wrists. The hempen rope bit into her flesh, snapping her mind into focus. What the thief said horrified her. Appalled her.

Intrigued her.

"Wait just a minute!" Once more, she kicked large Bob's abused shin and wrestled around to face Coop, flinging her arms free of the rope. Annoyance pinched the boss's lips, but Lorna was riding high on the sudden deliverance laid before her. "Be perfectly clear, sir. You mean to sell my brother's body?"

"Yeah, that's right. Now turn around like a good ewe and let me tie you up. I wouldn't argue with a third quarron, so don't make me do somefin unfortunate, eh?"

The threat hadn't much weight behind it, but who knew what these miscreants were capable of? Lorna licked her lips, recognizing a moment of decision was upon her. This was a group of thieves, she told herself, not murderers. If Coop and his gang meant her violence, they'd have done it already—wouldn't they?

Squeezing her eyes shut, Lorna summoned the image of her little brother. Daniel relied upon her. She'd sworn to do whatever it took to provide for and protect him. And so she would. The decision made, a strange calm settled over her.

Pretty Lem hopped to the driver's seat and took the reins from Daft Jemmy. The remaining men and the dog clambered into the bed with their frightful cargo, leaving room on the front bench for Coop. And Lorna, if she got her way. "Bob, help me into the wagon, please," she instructed her burly captor. She strode the short distance to the wagon, leaving a protesting Coop to trail in her wake.

"What in the bleedin', blazin' hells is this? Bob, don't you lift a finger to help her."

Lorna turned on a heel and shot Coop a quelling look. "Thomas's body belongs to his family. If anyone is going to sell it, it will be me."

Praise for *Honor Among Thieves*:

"Intriguing and unique, with likable, human characters ... mixed with competition, sexually charged scenes, and danger, this latest from Boyce is highly recommended for historical romance lovers."—Library Journal

"...a romantic version of a very grim (or Grimm) fairytale where the danger and horror of the journey is balanced by the exquisite and hard-fought peace of the ending."—Heroes and Heartbreakers

"...an unflinching look at the violent part of the Regency rarely seen. Boyce's prose is magnificently gritty and heartfelt, imbuing this romantic suspense with the perfect mix of light to calm the darkness ... "—Erica Monroe, USA Today Bestselling Author

For more books by Elizabeth Boyce, check out:

Once an Heiress

Praise for *Once an Heiress:*

"*Once an Heiress* combines everything readers love about historical romance with a twisting, suspenseful story that will have you on the edge of your seat ... I loved every second of *Once an Heiress*—it had the intrigue I love about historical romance combined with an excellent storyline that kept me on my toes."—The Romance Reviews

"If you like historical romances with a strong heroine that doesn't stick to society rules and a scarred hero with a wonderful hidden heart then you will like *Once an Heiress* by Elizabeth Boyce."—Harlequin Junkie

Once an Innocent

Praise for *Once an Innocent*:

"*Once an Innocent* by Elizabeth Boyce is a fantastic espionage romance that has some surprising action and gripping drama. If you are a 007 fan, you will be entertained by this novel."—The Romance Reviews

In the mood for more Crimson Romance?
Check out *The Duplicitous Debutante* by Becky Lower at
CrimsonRomance.com.

Printed in the United States
By Bookmasters